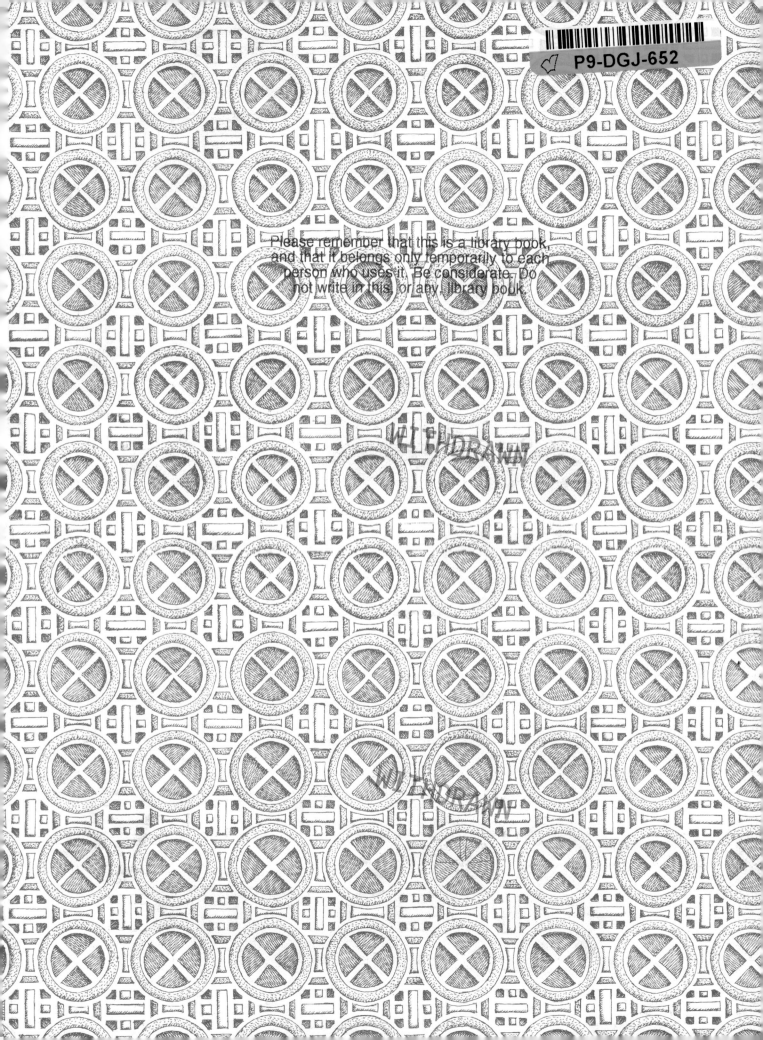

Anglo-Saxon
Mythology, Migration & Magic

Tony Linsell

Anglo-Saxon
Mythology, Migration & Magic

Tony Linsell

Includes
The Anglo-Saxon *Rune Poem*
with illustrations by
Brian Partridge

Anglo-Saxon Books

First published 1994 by
Anglo-Saxon Books
25 Malpas Drive
Pinner
Middlesex HA5 1DQ
England

Printed by
The Amadeus Press
Huddersfield
Yorkshire
England

Part of this book was published in 1992 as *Anglo-Saxon Runes*.
The text has been substantially revised and expanded for this edition.

Copyright Anglo-Saxon Books

ISBN 1-898281-09-2

Acknowledgements

My thanks to Brian Partridge for producing a superb collection of pen and ink drawings which are reproduced here at full size. I first saw his work at a 'Brotherhood of Ruralists' exhibition and thought it well suited to the sort of thing I had in mind for a set of Anglo-Saxon rune cards. He agreed to produce thirty-one illustrations which he thought would take him about three months to complete. Two years later the task was complete. The wait was well worthwhile.

Thanks to Stephen Pollington and Wendy Musker for their tips and advice. Last, thanks to Pearl for her help with the publication of this book.

Contents

Contents

Foreword

What follows is a mix of fact and speculation. The extensive use of 'probably', 'possibly', 'may' and 'perhaps' should make it clear where factual information ends and speculation begins. Very little information is available about life in heathen England, which is mainly due to it being an oral society. A written history began when Christianity was introduced during the 7th century but, for various obvious reasons, the Church did not wish to keep alive knowledge of heathen customs and festivals, and as a result much of the information we have is provided by writers who reveal information about heathen life in passing. Tacitus had no such reservations when he recorded nearly all the information we have about early Germanic society in *Germania*; much of the information given here about the early period comes from that source. The Prose and Poetic *Edda* by Snorri Sturluson is the source of much information about the mythological stories. John Kemble's *On Anglo-Saxon Runes* which first appeared in the journal Archaeologia for 1840 has also been very useful and several of the passages quoted here have been taken from Kemble's work. *The History of the English Church and People* by Bede contains useful information as does much Old English verse. (Highly recommended modern books are, *Spellcraft: Old English Heroic Legends*, and *Looking for the Lost Gods of England*, both by Kathleen Herbert.)

Several academic books are available on the subject of runes but most of the authors, perhaps sensibly, refrain from speculating on the magical meanings and uses of runes. However, one to be recommended is *An Introduction to English Runes* by R. I. Page. Non-academic books tend to be speculative, or inspirational, and most concern themselves with Scandinavian runes or Germanic runes in their earliest known form.

Those who wish to learn to read runes will probably find my rune cards helpful. The thirty cards, which carry smaller versions of the illustrations used in this book, are accompanied by an extensive information and instruction booklet.

One of the aims of this book is to give readers an insight into how the heathen values and way of life of the Anglo-Saxons survived into the Christian period.

Problems of terminology have arisen concerning the need to differentiate between male and female witches. I have decided to use witch for the female and wizard for the male. Some readers may feel uncomfortable with the use of 'wizard' instead of 'wicca', 'witch', 'male witch', 'shaman', or 'priest'. I too have my reservations but, for various reasons, the alternatives also give rise to difficulties and are probably even less suitable. Another choice had to be made between 'heathen' and 'pagan' but that was less difficult because although they both have similar meanings, 'heathen' is an English word whereas 'pagan' is from the Latin 'paganus'.

Because of the wide scope of the book it has not been possible to examine each area in great depth but hopefully the reader will find some information, and speculation, that is both new and interesting. One of my aims has been to demonstrate that the Anglo-Saxons have their own ancient traditions and folklore, and that they are as interesting as those of other cultures.

Germanic, Greek, Roman and Celtic heathen traditions are for the most part parallel, with the many similarities between them being mainly due to their common origins. Both the English/Anglo-Saxon (Germanic) and Celtic traditions have something to offer but in Britain British-Celtic history has, unfortunately, often been promoted as if it were English history. The popular perceptions this has created do not accord with the evidence. Just as Celts would find it objectionable if their folklore and ancient culture were described as a branch of English tradition, so the English are justified in taking exception to the current fashionable belief that almost every Anglo-Saxon festival, custom and art form is of Celtic origin or inspiration. That belief is mistaken, and it is to be hoped that this book will encourage those interested in such matters to look to early English history and early English society for clues to the origin of Anglo-Saxon traditions, institutions, and folklore. Another aim has been to make more people aware of a fascinating period of history.

Notes

In Old English the word *man* was not gender specific and should not be taken as being so here. Likewise *gods* includes *goddesses*.

The abbreviations C.E. (common era) and B.C.E. (before common era) are used instead of A.D. (anno Domini) and B.C. (before Christ).

O.E. is an abbreviation of Old English.

The term heathen (O.E. *hæþen*) is used throughout instead of *pagan* (Latin *paganus*).

The words *futhorc* and *futhark* are the English and German equivalents of the word *alphabet*, which is made up of the first two Greek letters *alpha* and *beta*. *Futhorc* represents the first six runes of the twenty-nine rune Anglo-Saxon Futhorc, and *futhark* represents the first six runes of both the twenty-four rune Germanic Elder Futhark and the sixteen rune Norse or Younger Futhark. A look at the table on page 57 will make this clear.

The early English came to be known as Anglo-Saxons but in our day that term means people of English origin wherever they may live in the world, and whatever their attachment to the country in which they live.

The letters æ, þ and ð are used in written Old English (Æ, Þ and Ð). Æ is called *ash* and has the same sound as *a* in ash. Þ is called *thorn*, after the name of the rune from which it is derived, and it has the sound *th* as in thorn. As a general rule ð (*eth*), which also represents *th*, is interchangeable with þ.

The stanzas of the *Rune Poem* have been reproduced in a manuscript style similar to that used in England during the 9th and 10th centuries. Some of the letter shapes will be unfamiliar but in order to help the reader appreciate that there is not as great a difference between Old English and Modern English as might first appear, the poem has also been reproduced in the commonly used 'edited' form. If all the letters are pronounced, many of the words will become recognizable. The letters *sc* together are pronounced *sh* as in ship. Some other letters are also used differently in Old English but that is beyond the scope of this note.

Introduction

The Engle were a Germanic tribe who lived in the southern part of the Jutland peninsula. (See maps on pages 37 & 43) The name of the tribe was recorded in Latin as *Anglii*, which later became *Angles*. To add to the confusion the Engle, along with the Jutes and Frisians, were known collectively to the people in Britain and to the south of the Rhine as Saxons. The Saxons were in fact a confederation of tribes who lived to the south of the Engle but because the fame of the Saxons had spread far and wide due to their seaborne raids along the East coast of Britain and the Atlantic coast of Europe, and because the Germanic tribes of North West Europe shared a similar appearance, culture and language, they all came to be known to outsiders as Saxons. The reason for the introduction of the term Anglo-Saxon is uncertain but it was either used to differentiate between the Engle and other Saxons, or to distinguish the *Saxons* (Engle, Jutes, Frisians, Saxons) who migrated to Britain from those who stayed behind and who were called Old Saxons. In more recent times the term Anglo-Saxon has been used to describe the mixture of Germanic people who migrated to Britain during the fifth, sixth and seventh centuries A.D. and who then, about 1,000 years later became part of a new wave of migration which resulted in the formation of Anglo-Saxon societies in North America and Australasia.

As a result of various developments in the language and its pronunciation, the *Engle* became the *English*. It is probable that the English were by far the largest group of Anglo-Saxon migrants to Britain, and because of that, and the eventual dominance of their kingdoms in Britain, all the Germanic migrants and other people who became absorbed into their society and culture came to be known as the English, although sometimes the names 'Saxon' or 'Anglo-Saxon' were used. The land in which they lived was called England and the language they spoke was English. That language, now called Old English, has evolved through Middle English into the English we speak today (Modern English).

The Anglo-Saxons went to Britain as heathens and took with them their institutions, their Gods, and the confident and positive outlook on life that their beliefs fostered. More than 150 years after their migration to Britain began, Augustine landed in Kent (597) and set in motion the process which saw the nominal conversion of the English people to Christianity. That process did not involve an abrupt end to one system of belief and the beginning of another, it was instead a gradual take-over of the existing institutions and the adoption and modification of many heathen beliefs and customs. Part of the success of the Church was due to its ability to adapt to local conditions and to assimilate local customs, folklore and beliefs. In this way the Church preserved and promoted as Christian much that had roots in the heathen past. This is not to say that the Church was not hostile to the Old Religion or that it did not discriminate against or punish those who indulged in heathen practices. However it should not be thought that practices associated with the Spanish inquisition or the witch-burning of later times occurred in England during the first millennium.

That the Anglo-Saxon migrants were able to merge into one nation was due to the similarity of their language and culture. Even the Welsh, against whom the English fought, were a culturally related people. Although it is probable that few of the Welsh were ethnic Celts, most had assimilated something of Celtic culture, which had the same origins as, and many similarities to, Germanic, Greek and Latin cultures. Ethnic Celts were described by Roman writers as being tall, fair-haired and blue-eyed. In view of this it is surprising that so many of those who are so strident in proclaiming, what they believe to be, their Celtic ancestry, fail to fit the Roman description, and those that do are often the descendants of Scandinavian, mainly Norwegian, settlers.

When the Danes and other Scandinavians settled in England they were eventually absorbed into English society and its culture. After the early period of invasion and warfare the two peoples lived, for the most part, peacefully side by side and the Danes gradually adopted the English language, which was similar to their own. The process of assimilation gave rise to some changes in the English way of life and introduced some Norse words into the English vocabulary. The most important consequence of the linguistic compromises that took place during that period of assimilation, was that English was simplified. For example word endings were dropped and word order was changed. These fundamental changes were far more important than the comparatively few additions to English vocabulary.

The Normans were 'Northmen' who, under the leadership of Rolf Ganger, a Norwegian Viking, went to north-west Gaul in 911 and, after an initial defeat and conversion to Christianity, established the Duchy of Normandy. It may have been because they were so different in appearance from the native population that the Northmen felt able to assimilate Frankish culture and language without it threatening their group identity. When the Normans invaded England, 155 years later, they formed a comparatively small ruling elite. It was perhaps because of their similar appearance to the English that they used their adopted Frankish culture and language as a method for preserving their identity. The main influence they had on the English language was to greatly expand its vocabulary by introducing foreign (Norman French) words into it. It was this that gave rise to much of the confusion we have in Modern English with, for example, different rules for spelling different foreign loan words.

Because Norman French was used by the political, administrative, legal and religious elites, the foreign words became entrenched in those areas of activity and among certain classes. However, the great mass of the people went on speaking English and the language continued to evolve as it had before.

Many foreign loan words are very useful, fit well into English and enrich it. However, many are ugly and sit uncomfortably. Perhaps if there were a greater appreciation that the unity and beauty of English (what is left of it) is being destroyed, and an awareness that Greek and Latin words are not superior to English words, some thought would be given to the matter of compatibility when new words are created, as they constantly are. It would be better to use English root words as they are generally more readily understood by English speakers. New words enrich a language but they need not be of foreign origin to do so.

Old English is a beautiful language, as is Latin, and it can express much with few words. (Not something to be welcomed by those who prefer jargon, and the use of long words where small ones will do, in the belief that it makes them, and what they say, sound more important.) Mixing Latin, Greek and English together spoils them all. The King James' Bible contains very few loan words but is none the worse for that.

The Norman invaders of the 11th century, while fewer in number than the Danes, were the cause of far greater long-term political and linguistic change. However, despite the deep changes, the Normans remained primarily a small ruling elite which was eventually absorbed into the English population.

While the elite used Norman French for the affairs of state, the ordinary English people continued to use English, which evolved into Middle English. The interest in Chaucer is due, in large part, to the fact that he chose to write in English instead of Norman French or Latin.

Since 1066 there has been no successful invasion of England and, until the beginning of the 20th century, no significant migration of peoples into England that could not easily be absorbed into English society and the English population.

During the late 16th and early 17th centuries, English adventurers, explorers and colonists laid the foundations of the English Empire which was later to become known as the British Empire. For the next three hundred years English people went overseas and created new societies which were greatly influenced by the one they had left behind. Their institutions, including the political and legal systems, were for the most part English, as were their culture and attitudes. It was natural that in different environments those societies should evolve in different ways and that the descendants of those settlers should identify with their new society and cease to regard themselves as English. However, they are still Anglo-Saxons, as an increasing number of them are beginning to appreciate. The early history of the English people is part of their history.

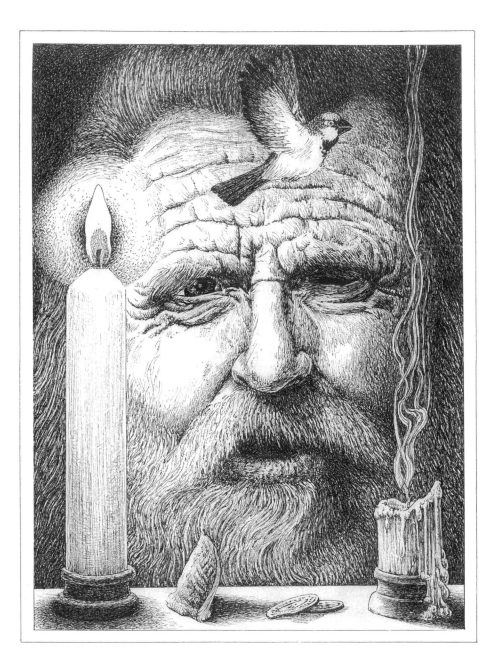

The Creation

Allfather is very strong and full of might. He lives through all time and governs
all things. He is the father of the heavens and the earth and all that is in them.
When he made man he gave him a soul that can live on and need never die
though the body will drop to dust or burn to ashes.

Night is the greatest of mysteries; she is the past and the future.
All of creation came from her womb and to her embrace it will return.

Allfather took on the form of Twilight and had a child by Night;
it was a son named Space.

Allfather had a second child by Night;
it was a daughter named Earth.

Allfather took on the form of Dawn and had a third child by Night;
it was a son named Day.

The first world was one of great heat and great cold. The north was full of ice and
frost and gusts of wind. The south was full of fire and sparks and glowing embers.
Where the soft air of the heat met the harsh frost of the cold the air was as mild as
windless air and the ice began to sweat, and life appeared in the drops of running
fluid. From out of the ice and mud there came a giant called Clay and while he slept
there grew under his left arm a man and a woman, and from them came the first race
of men that was given the Earth to live in. Then one of the giant's legs had a son with
the other and that is where the family of frost giants came from.

Next to appear from the ice was a cow called Nourisher. Four rivers of milk
sprang from her teats and from these the giant fed. Nourisher licked the salty ice and
by the evening she had uncovered some hair. On the second day she uncovered a
head and on the third day the whole being in the form of a man was revealed. His
name was Tuist and he was handsome, tall and strong. He had a son named Mann,
who had three sons by the daughter of a frost giant. The first son was Wisdom; the
second Will; the third Holiness. The three sons fell out with Clay and killed him. So
vast was his size, and so great were the torrents of blood that poured from his
wounds, that all the Frost giants were drowned; all except one who escaped with his
wife in a boat.

The three sons of Mann made the world from the corpse of the giant. From his
blood came the sea and the lakes; from his flesh, the earth; from his bones, the
mountains; from his jaws, teeth and broken bones came rocks and pebbles; from his
hair, the trees. Maggots came to life in his flesh and the gods gave them the
appearance of men and human understanding. This was the origin of the dwarfs who
live in the earth and rocks. They are very wise and the most skilful of craftsmen.

From the giant's skull the sky was formed. It was placed over the earth and under
each corner the three sons placed a dwarf. These are known as North, East, South

and West. The brains of the giant were flung into the sky and formed clouds. Higher than the clouds were flung sparks and embers and these became the heavenly lights. The position of the stars was fixed and the lights that wandered at will were given paths on which to travel.

Night, and her son Day, ride around the earth on two horses. Night rides first on a horse called Frosty-mane and every morning the foam from his bit covers the earth as dew. Day rides on a horse called Shining-mane and the sunlight glistens on his golden hair.

When Wisdom, Will and Holiness had finished making the world they travelled about it to inspect their work. While they were walking together by the sea they found two trees that had been washed ashore. The brothers made a man from one tree, and a woman from the other. The man was called Ash and the woman was called Elm. Wisdom gave them each a soul and life. Will gave them understanding and movement. Holiness gave them the power of speech and the senses of sight, touch, smell, taste and hearing. From Ash and Elm came the people of Allfather and the Gods looked on them with favour.

The Gods

Sunnandæg. The first day is for Sun the fiery light that is drawn through the heavens by a team of horses. Sun rises in the East, turning frost giants into stone, then hurries across the sky chased by a snarling wolf who catches her at the edge of the western sky and swallows her whole. Then Night rides out and covers the Earth until Sun, the companion of Day, escapes and once again casts her bright light over the earth. By Sun we measure a year.

Turn towards the rising sun and bow humbly nine times, and then say these words:

> Eastwards I stand, for favours I pray.
> I pray the great Measurer, I pray the mighty Sun,
> I pray the holy Protector of the heavenly kingdom.
> Earth I pray and sky, and Frig the Mother of Man,
> and heaven's might and high hall, that by the grace
> of the Sky-Father I may speak this charm and by
> my firm will raise up these crops for our worldly use,
> fill this earth by steadfast faith, make beautiful these grasslands;
> as Woden said that he would have favours on earth who was
> open handed and bold, according to the will of the Gods.

Then turn three times with the course of the sun, then stretch yourself along the ground and say three times, 'Sun, Sky, Rain, Earth'. Then stretch out your arms to embrace the earth, and say these words:

> Praise be to Ing the Green Man. Praise be to Frig, Mother of Earth.
> Praise be to Irminsul the pillar of creation.
> Look with favour on those who are dependent upon this land
> and bring forth bountiful crops for them all.

Monandæg. The second day is for Moon the silver sphere that lights the night sky with its ghostly gleam. Moon, the companion of Night, waxes and wanes, and we call this time a month.

Tiwesdæg. The third day is for Tiw.
Allfather created the gods of the shining stronghold that is Heaven, and bestowed on each of them great powers. Tiw was the first of the gods of Heaven; the Sky Father; the God of Brightness. It is from Tiw the great warrior and God of Battle, that warriors seek courage and strength. He is protector and provider; the God of Order, Law and Justice. Tiw watches over the assembly of the people that is called the Moot or Thing.

Wodnesdæg. The fourth day is for Woden.
Woden is the God of Wisdom, the God of War, and God of the Dead. He is a wizard and a healer and has the power of prophecy. In his quest for knowledge and understanding he gave an eye and hung from Irminsul the Pillar of the Universe, for nine days and nights, wounded by a spear. He is wise beyond the understanding of men and from Woden, the one-eyed god, came the runes. It is to Woden, God of Wisdom, that the wise look for truth and knowledge. It is to Woden, the God of War, that warriors look for victory. It is to Woden, God of the Slain, that the dying look for comfort. In his search for lost souls he comes to the Middle Enclosure, the world of men, and moves stealthily across the earth in cloak and hood. On dark and stormy nights he rides across the sky with the Valkyries, the Daughters of Night.

Þunresdæg. The fifth day is for Thunor.
Thunor is very strong and full of vigour. The dwarfs made him a mighty hammer called Crusher, and a pair of iron gloves with which to hold it. They also made him a belt of power with which he can double his strength. Thunor uses these gifts to help him protect Heaven and the world of men. He is God of the Weather and the Seasons. He drives his chariot over the storm clouds and throws thunderbolts from the mountain tops. From his chariot he can hurl Crusher to earth, fell an oak, and have the hammer return to his hand.

Thunor cares for the well-being of men and helps them build and cultivate. He is at the rite for the naming of children, and at weddings, and the cremation or burial of the dead. His presence is symbolized by the hammer and he is with those who wear it.

Frigedæg. The sixth day is for Frig.
Earth is the daughter of Night. She cares for us and provides us with all that we need for a full and happy life, just as she provided for those who went before. It is for us to use her ample harvest wisely. We are wardens of Earth and we must care for her so that she can care for us and those who come after us.

Frig is Earth and of Earth. She is her own daughter and is known by many names. Frig is Mother Earth and she is the Goddess of Fertility and Love. She brings us the fruits of the earth and of our loins. She is Goddess of the Harvest and the Mother of Men. The Wise seek her help in many things. Frig, like her companion Woden, has the power of prophecy.

Erce, Erce, Erce, Mother of Earth,
may the Mother of the Harvest grant us
fields sprouting and thriving,
flourishing and bountiful,
bright shafts of millet-crops,
and of broad barley-crops,
and of white wheat-crops,
and of all the crops of the earth.
May the mighty and everlasting Allfather,
and the Gods in Heaven,
grant us that our produce be safe against every foe,
and secure against every harm,
from witchcraft sown throughout the land.
Now I pray to the mighty Creator of this world
that no wicce may be so cunning, and no wicca so crafty
that they can upset the words thus spoken.

Hail to thee, Earth, Mother of Men.
Be fruitful in the sky's embrace,
filled with food for the use of mankind.

Sæternesdæg. The seventh day is for our ancestors.

Many have gone before and many will follow. Those who went before live on in our bodies and our memories. Those who will follow live in our bodies and our hopes. We are the meeting place for past and future. We must keep alive the memory of the dead, so that the unborn can know and remember them. Remember their names and their deeds and yours in turn will be remembered.

Allfather has no form but that of the universe which is the emblem of his existence. The emblem of the universe is Irminsul the great Yew, the pillar of the universe; its roots and branches reach into all the worlds of creation.

The emblem of Tiw is the sword.

The emblems of Woden are the ring and the spear.

The emblem of Thunor is the hammer.

The emblems of Frig are the sheaf of corn and the amber necklace.

The emblems of our forebears are our bodies.

The Wise Ones, both the wicca and the wicce, were the wardens of the Old Ways and its rituals. They were the keepers of starcraft, runecraft, lorecraft and wortcraft and they guided many through the darkness of the future and healed bodies and minds. The wiccan were wardens of the holy places where mighty trees were the walls and the glorious sky the roof. Water, be it in spring, pool or well, is the water of Wisdom, Destiny, and Death. The idols, and other emblems of the Old Ways, give comfort and bring the gods closer to those who invoke their help or give them praise.

Irminsul and the Seven Worlds

Around the earth in a ring are four seas; two fresh and two salt. Along the outer shores of the seas the gods gave the giants a land to live in but not all the giants are to be found there; some live in the depths of the earth, while others can be found in caves high in the mountains, or beneath the waves in the deep sea.

Away from the ring of sea the gods built a stronghold from the eyebrows of the dead giant, and they called it Middangeard, (the Middle Enclosure). This is Earth the land of men and it is midway between the world of the gods and Hel, the realm of death and darkness. The gods then built a stronghold with many fine halls for themselves and their kindred; it is called Heaven. The route from earth to Heaven is over a very strong bridge made with great skill and cunning. It is called Shimmering Rainbow and it is guarded by Hama, the White God, who never sleeps. He sits at the edge of Heaven watching like a hawk, both night and day, and listens for the smallest sound. If Hama detects the faintest threat to Heaven he will blow Echoing Horn, which will be heard in every part of every one of the seven worlds.

Each day those gods who are not travelling in other worlds ride over Shimmering Rainbow and meet by Irminsul, the great yew, that is the pillar of the universe. It has very strong roots and its branches tower into the sky. Irminsul stretches into every part of the universe and connects the worlds of the Gods, Light Elves, Dark Elves, Men, Dwarfs, Giants, and the Dead. Beyond the Realm of the Dead there is fire and heat. Beyond Heaven there is ice and cold.

Irminsul has three long roots. One passes into the World of the Dead, another into the World of Frost Giants and the third into the World of the Gods. Under the root that goes down to the World of the Dead is the spring called Roaring Cauldron and nearby lives a dragon called Devourer of Corpses. Under the root that turns towards the World of Frost Giants is the spring that is guarded by the god Mimir. Those who drink its waters are given great wisdom and understanding. Such was Woden's thirst for knowledge that he gave an eye for a drink from that spring.

Under the root that rises into Heaven is the spring of Destiny. It is by this water that the gods meet each day. Near by live the three Daughters of Night called Wyrd, Metod and Sculd. They are the Spinner, Measurer and Cutter of the threads of life that are woven into the Web of Wyrd. The first sister, Wyrd, spins the thread and it is she who determines its quality. Metod measures the thread and determines its length. Sculd cuts the thread and by the nature of the cut, be it clean or ragged, she determines the manner of our death. We know these midnight women, the Wyrd Sisters, as Past, Present and Future. Each day they draw water from the Spring of Destiny and return to their dark cave where they spin and weave the destinies of men. On the night of a full moon they gather round the pool and call down the shimmering light into the sparkling water. Wyrd is everywhere and all the inhabitants of all the worlds are within her power.

The Valkyries, the fierce Daughters of Night, ride across the dark and stormy skies on their black steeds, and present a dreadful sight to those who see their staring, hideous eyes, and hear the din of their hunt. They are able to bring defeat or victory in battle and they weave the Web of Victory from the guts of men on a bloodstained frame of spears. The shuttle is an arrow, and the warp is weighted with men's skulls. These mighty women ride to the field of battle and select those who are to die. When the fury of battle is spent, they appear on the crimson field among the dead as wolves and ravens. Then, blotched with blood, and with sparks flashing from their spear points, they ride away with the souls of the dead.

Fiercewolf, the World Serpent, and Hel

Deep in the great forest, to the east of the land of men, live giant women with magical powers. One of those women, who is very old, gave birth to the two wolves who chase Sun and Moon across the sky. Many years later the crone had three more children by a giant. The first was called Fiercewolf, and he grew larger and more ferocious each day. The second was a monstrous serpent which grew more ugly and venomous. The third was a daughter, named Hel, and she was black in parts and looked grim and shadowy.

The gods knew of these children and the threat they posed to Heaven and Earth so they went to the forest in search of them. When they found the serpent they threw it into the deep sea where it grew so large it circled the earth, and its head touched its tail. Hel was sent to the seventh world, the realm of the dead, and there she rules a world surrounded by high walls and secured by heavy gates, so that those who enter never return. She lives in a damp hall called Chill Wind, where Glimmering Misfortune hangs from the walls. Her plate is called Starvation; her knife Famine; her door Ruin; her bed Pestilence.

The gods tried to capture Fiercewolf, but he was very large and strong, and all the fetters they put on him were easily broken. They went away and made a very strong chain, and when they returned they asked the wolf to test his strength against it. Fiercewolf looked at the chain carefully and accepted the challenge. At his very first attempt he easily broke free. The gods went away and made a chain twice as strong as the one before, and asked the wolf to test his strength again. They told him he would gain great fame if he could break free from such a strong fetter. The wolf thought about it carefully and decided that, if he were to achieve fame, he would have to face danger. The chain looked very strong, but he had grown in size and strength since the last challenge, so he agreed to have the chain put on him. The wolf struggled and strained so hard that the chain shattered and flew off. The gods were worried that they might never be able to restrain the wolf, so they sent a messenger to the Dwarfs who live deep underground. Those most excellent craftsmen made a fetter from six things: the roots of a mountain; the breath of a fish; the noise of a cat's footstep; the beard of a woman; the sinews of a bear; the spittle of a bird.

The messenger returned with a fetter that looked like the web of a spider. The gods challenged the wolf to be bound once more, but Fiercewolf thought it must be a trick and snarled at them, and said there was no fame to be gained from breaking such a flimsy fetter. The gods said that if he was afraid they would promise to free him if he could not do so himself. Fiercewolf did not believe them, but he did not want to be thought a coward, so he agreed to the challenge provided one of them, as a token of good faith, placed a hand in the wolf's mouth. The gods looked at each other wondering what to do. Tiw stepped forward and placed his hand between the wolf's powerful jaws. The other gods bound the wolf, who then began to struggle, but the more he struggled the tighter the fetter became. All the gods laughed; all except Tiw who lost his hand. The gods pulled the fetter tight and fastened its end to a large rock. Fiercewolf snarled and frothed at the mouth but the gods forced a large sword upright between his jaws and left him howling as a warning to others who might threaten them.

Migration

The people of Allfather lived in the Middle Enclosure by the waters of the Black Sea. They had a common language and symbols, called runes, by which they represented the sun and the earth and the mysteries of this life and what lies beyond it. Those mystical and secret shapes were used to invoke the forces of nature and the gods who controlled them.

With the passing of time the people divided into many tribes, each of which developed small differences in custom and dialect. As the tribes moved into new lands, some to the east and some to the west, they came to form two main language groups each of which spoke a slightly different tongue. We call one of these groups the Centum and the other the Satem. From the Centum came the Germans, Greeks, Latins (Romans), Celts, Tocharians, Hittites and Albanians. From the Satem came the Balts, Indics, Iranians, Armenians and Slavs. They came to call the Gods by different names and worship them in different ways but they all gave praise to Sun and Moon, and the Sky Father and the Earth Mother.

One of the tribes, the Aesir, migrated to the north-west and followed great rivers and passed through vast forests and marshes. They travelled for many generations and faced great challenges and dangers together, and in doing so their sense of community and common purpose was strengthened. In the North they came to the land of the Vanir, a people who worshipped gods of the sea and of the earth. The Aesir found land for themselves and built houses, grew crops and raised cattle.

The Aesir were named after their Gods who were Gods of the sky, wisdom and war. The Vanir likewise shared the name of their Gods who were great workers of magic and Gods of fertility. When the two peoples fought against each other in the first war, they called on their gods for help, and the Gods of wisdom and war were pitted against the Gods of fertility and magic. Much blood was spilt in the long conflict and the people, and their gods, became weary of war. A truce was called and the two sides met to discuss the causes of the conflict and to see if a peaceful settlement could be reached. They could not agree about the cause of the war but they decided to live together in peace, and as proof of their good faith they agreed to an exchange of leaders. The Vanir sent the Daughter of the Sea to teach her hosts skills of magic, and the Aesir sent Mimir, the guardian of the well of wisdom and understanding, to provide wise counsel for the Vanir. The gods sealed the agreement by spitting into a communal bowl, and from the spittle they made a being blessed with great wisdom and powers of magic.

After many generations of living in isolation in the land called Scania, the two peoples became one. All the people prospered and there were many tribes, and many children: Scania became the womb of nations.

Over three thousand years ago some of the tribes moved south across the sea to Jutland and then further south to the great northern plain that stretches from beyond the Rhine in the west to beyond the Vistula in the east. Some turned west and followed the flat, low-lying North Sea coast where they found a mixture of bog, marshland, heath and moorland. There were also areas of fertile land and in those places the people settled, and grew crops, and grazed cattle. Land at the mouth of the Wesser and the Ems was particularly good and many settlements sprang up there. The population grew, and as it did so people moved up the rivers seeking new lands.

Some tribes, on reaching the northern plain, turned east and passed along the fertile coastal plain to the River Oder. As in the west, some tribes settled when they found suitable land while others moved on. Some reached the Oder and followed that river south, and settled to the east of it. Many turned neither east nor west but headed south and arrived on the banks of the lower Elbe, where they made their home. That river was to become an important route into the central uplands, and beyond to the River Danube.

As the tribes spread out they adapted their way of life so as to survive and prosper in the various lands and climates they found. The conditions they experienced gave rise to changes in the way they built their houses, grew their crops and kept their animals. That in turn influenced the way their communities and language evolved. At first the differences from tribe to tribe were small but as they spread out across the great plain the communities became more distinctive. Like all peoples, they had to solve the problems of feeding, housing and defending themselves. Different surroundings and climate gave rise to various solutions to basically the same problems. Societies, like other living things, must adapt to their environment or perish.

Although the tribes developed different skills, customs and dialects, the sense of being one people was preserved by the gleemen and other story tellers who travelled widely and spread news about the goings on in far off places. In those oral societies history was recorded in poems, many of which were about battles and the deeds of famous warriors. Group identity was also strengthened by the contact they had, during the push south, with peoples who were different from them in appearance, culture and religion.

As periodic waves of migration brought more tribes south from Scania the fertile lands near to the northern seas became heavily settled . Areas of forest started to be cleared and there was an increase in movement along the river valleys towards the south-west. The great advance of the Northern people towards the central uplands took many generations to complete and as they went they pushed others before them. On reaching the higher ground they came into contact with Celtic societies who were unable to halt the advance or to prevent the people of Scania settling the land. The Celts had been a powerful military force in Europe and were responsible for many artistic and technological innovations. However, they were comparatively few in number and when they took control of large territories they could only do so as ruling elites. Eventually the ethnic Celts were lost in the vast populations they ruled.

Around 250 B.C.E., after a long period of consolidation and a growth in population, many of the Northern tribes renewed their advance into the Central Uplands and a new wave of migration began. The early movement was, as before, mostly south east along rivers that flowed from the uplands to the northern seas. When the tribes crossed the watershed, they travelled down the rivers flowing south-east to the Danube and the Black Sea. During the following 200 years the Northern peoples occupied, and took control of, most of the land between the Rhine and the Vistula, and the Danube and the Baltic. As they spread out across this vast territory they came to be described as Germans of the Sea, Germans of the Forest, and Germans of the Steppes. The Germans of the Sea gave praise to Ing, from whom they were descended, and among their number were the Engle, Friese, Eote and Seaxe (English Frisians, Jutes, and Saxons).

Language

The differences in dialect between the widespread Germanic peoples became great enough for three distinct language groups to be discerned. These can be called the Northern, Eastern and Western Germanic groups. The dialects of the people of the north developed through Norse into Danish, Icelandic, Norwegian, Swedish and Faroese. The dialects of the Eastern group, which were very similar to those of the Northern group, became Gothic, Vandalic, and Burgundian, and are now extinct. The dialects of the Western group became Frisian, English, Scots, Dutch, and German. (The first four of these are 'Ingraeonic' or North Sea Germanic.) When some of the tribes of the Western group moved further south, their language developed in a different way from that of the lowland Germans they left behind. The southern group, who came to inhabit the central uplands, called themselves Duesche (modern Deutsch), which means 'Men of the People'. Those who in English are commonly called 'Germans' are the Duesche and they are but one of the Germanic peoples and their language but one of the Germanic tongues.

The People

Although there were differences in custom and social organization among the Germanic peoples, the similarities were far greater. Germanic society was a warrior society based on self-sufficient communities which, at first, had little contact with non-Germanic peoples except as enemies in war. The Germans tended to have blue eyes, fair skin, fair or reddish hair, and they were taller and bigger than the people of the south. The men wore long woollen cloaks fastened with a brooch or thorn. Many women wore loose, sleeveless, outer garments, made from linen, which exposed part of their breasts. Boys and girls were brought up together and young women were able to match the strength of young men of their own age. Children were not pampered and grew up able to endure cold, damp and hardship. In some places, sexual activity before the age of twenty was considered scandalous and harmful to the development of a tall stature and fine physique. Once married no attempt was made to restrict the number of children and it was not their custom, as it was elsewhere, to kill girls at birth. A large number of kin gave one authority and social standing.

Houses and Settlements

The Germanic people tended to live in small self-sufficient settlements. Houses and farm buildings were constructed from timber and some had walls that were smeared with a clay that gave them a bright appearance. Although all buildings were made from timber, the layout and method of construction varied according to the climate and the nature of the land. Some settlements started as single farmsteads consisting of a small two-post building and assorted shelters. Where the farmers were successful larger houses were built close to the first, which might then be pulled down and the timber re-used. As the size of the family increased so additional houses and sheds for use as workshops or food stores were built nearby. If the land was well drained, wood-lined pits were built for the storage of grain but in other places it was stored in buildings with raised floors. Where the climate was mild, cattle and other animals were left in the open during the winter, but if it was very cold or wet the houses were made larger to provide a home for the farmer and his family at one end, and shelter for the livestock at the other. These buildings are known as longhouses and many of them were of the three-aisle type of construction. A widespread and common type of small building was the Grubenhauser or sunken building. These were built on well drained land around a flat bottomed pit of two feet, or more, in depth. The turf or thatch roofs on such buildings were supported at the high point by two upright posts and a ridge pole, while the bottom edge rested on the ground, or on a turf wall. They were used as small houses or workshops and offered greater protection against cold winds and snow than ground level structures. With the top soil removed a firm floor surface of chalk, clay or compressed gravel might be revealed. The hearth in earthen floored houses was situated either in the centre of the floor or in one corner. In some later buildings with ground level wooden floors over pits, the hearth was made of clay and stones laid on the wooden floorboards.

The people who lived in the flat marshy lands north of the mouth of the Rhine (The Netherlands), where there was often flooding, erected their houses and other buildings on man made mounds known as terpen. Some of the mounds were constructed of clay to a height of two or three feet so as to provide firm bases for buildings and areas on which to keep livestock when the surrounding land was flooded. Those mounds that were occupied for long periods gradually increased in height and area as a result of the accumulation of various forms of debris and rubbish and some stood six or seven feet high by the end of their period of occupation. A roughly circular terpen measuring about 500 feet from side to side might have ten to fifteen longhouses built on it.

Some of the sites on which the Germanic peoples built their settlements had been occupied earlier. It was usual for migrating people to make use of, and modify, the economic and military resources and structures of earlier inhabitants. In the frontier regions use was often made of existing hill-forts that had not been occupied for many years. The addition of a fence of wooden stakes to a ditch and mound defence-work could quickly provide a secure place of settlement. Good military positions often remain as such despite the passing of time and changes in technology and tactics. Likewise settlements tend to grow up near mountain passes, river fords and where tracks converge. Newcomers often find a settlement site as attractive as earlier occupants and for the same reasons.

Settlements founded by a large group of people were more likely to be planned and laid out around a central open space or along a street whereas settlements that grew gradually, perhaps from a single homestead, had buildings and animal pens arranged in a less systematic way. Most buildings were constructed on an east-west axis so that one of the long walls faced south towards the sun and allowed more light to enter through the doorway and small shuttered windows.

Some settlements failed and were deserted while others thrived and became populated by several hundred people. The successful ones became the focal point of a stable farming community and some became centres for the manufacture of various artefacts such as pottery and iron products. Many have developed into the present-day towns and villages of northern Europe.

The Distribution of Land

Much of the central area of Germany was covered with forest and marsh land. Clearing such land for farming was by necessity a communal effort so, when the clearance was completed, the land tended to be held in common by those who had helped clear it and was shared out by a means that was fair and agreeable to everyone. The sharing of land, and of similar conditions and problems, helped to promote community spirit. Status within the group was achieved not by accumulating land but by demonstrating loyalty, generosity and courage. Some display of material wealth was possible through the acquisition and breeding of livestock which was not held in common. This is probably the reason why cattle (O.E. *feoh*) came to represent wealth and why wealth is represented by the rune *feoh*.

The yearly allocation of arable land was usually made to kindred groups, each group being allocated strips from several different parts of the common arable land so as to ensure that all shared similar rewards and hardships. In some places the kin worked the land together and shared the produce while in others they sub-divided the land amongst themselves with the size of the allotments being adjusted to reflect the social rank of the individuals concerned.

Crops and Husbandry

Most settlements had some form of defence system which usually consisted of a ditch and mound with a fence of strong wooden stakes. Ideally the arable and pasture land encircled the settlement to give a clear view of the surrounding country side and good warning of the approach of strangers. Such a layout was also the most economical in terms of travelling time between house and field. The cultivated land around large settlements was extensive and it would have been time-consuming, if the settlement had not been in a central position, to drive a team of oxen out to the furthest field each morning and back each evening, especially as the days were short during the early part of the year when the fields were ploughed.

The boundaries of fields were often marked by ditches and earth mounds but to these were added the stones that were gradually cleared from the field during preparation of the soil for sowing. On sloping ground the fields might be terraced or run lengthways across the slope to lessen soil erosion from running water.

As the Germanic peoples advanced south they took possession of many existing field systems from which the former inhabitants had either fled or been driven. Where fields had physical boundaries, such as ditches or piles of stones, they were retained and modified slowly but any extension to the system was carried out in a way known to, or traditional to, the new owners.

The distribution of land between arable, meadow, and pasture varied, as did the size and shape of the fields, from place to place according to climate and the nature of the land. A single farmstead in North West Germany with fields totalling thirty-five acres, might have only seven to ten acres of arable with the remainder being a mixture of pasture and hay meadow.

Two basic types of plough were used to prepare the ground for the sowing crops. The first, an ard, used a wooden or iron share to scratch or dig a furrow and push the displaced soil to each side. The other type of plough had a share that pushed the soil to one side and in doing so turned it over. A piece of timber known as a mouldboard was sometimes fitted to the plough to assist the turning of the soil. The ploughs were drawn by teams of oxen and it was found to be more economical in time and effort to plough long furrows so as to reduce the number of times the animals had to be turned. As a result the fields tended to be long and narrow. Such a system also reduced the amount of unploughed land required at the end of each field for turning the oxen.

The main cereal crop was barley which was used to make bread and beer. Oats and rye were also harvested but in much smaller quantities. There were vegetable crops such as cabbage, carrots, beans, and peas. Apples, pears, cherries and plums were grown, and in the south there were apricots and peaches. Bilberries, blackberries, elderberries, raspberries and strawberries were cultivated and gathered, as were many herbs for use in cooking and medicines. Common herbs included caraway, dill, garlic, and parsley. Some plants were grown for use as dyes. Flax was grown for linseed oil and the fibre used to make linen.

There was no division of pasture-land but there may have been restrictions on the number of sheep or cattle which could be grazed there. Pigs fed on the forest edges where they ate acorns and beech-mast in winter. The farm animals provided, in addition to meat, milk for cheese and yoghurt; wool and hide for clothing, blankets, belts and shoes; fat for burning in lamps; bone for making combs, needles and other implements. Most utensils and artefacts were made from wood, leather or clay.

Spinning and weaving were highly developed skills and each settlement or family produced cloth for its own use. The quality varied according to the use to which it was to be put but it was possible to produce very fine cloth on a simple loom. Pottery for everyday use was simple in material, technique and design, and most of it was made by members of a household as and when it was required.

Government

The kindred groups were mostly independent and self-governing in time of peace but in war they joined together and elected a leader (king) for the duration of the conflict. Practices varied and sometimes it was necessary to have a joint leadership. At first it was the custom for all warriors to be eligible for election but among some tribes it became the practice to select the leader from one family and eventually the king remained as such for life. Whatever the method of selection the chieftain did not have absolute power and he could be overruled by a council of leading men among whom there would probably have been at least one wizard. As the chieftain had no power to compel warriors to fight he had to lead by example and show skill and courage in battle.

The council of leading men were given power to make decisions on many matters which affected all of the people, but on important issues the council discussed the matter before putting a recommendation before an assembly of warriors who were able to discuss the proposal and then adopt or reject it. This assembly of warriors came to be known as a 'Thing' or 'Moot'. The meeting took place just before the full moon or shortly after the new moon, these being considered the best times to make decisions or start new ventures. All warriors, with the exception of those who had shown cowardice in battle, were entitled to attend the moot and they did so fully armed to show their right to carry arms and their ability to fight if necessary. When a matter had to be decided those opposed to the proposal shouted their disapproval and those in favour clashed their spears. A warrior who gave his support to a proposal was honour bound to act in support of it. Thus if he favoured a proposed act of war he was expected to fight.

The moot was able to consider the criminal offences of treachery, desertion, cowardice and sodomy. Those found guilty of any of the first three offences were hung from a tree but the punishment for sodomy was to be bound and pressed down into a bog under a wicker hurdle. The executions were carried out by wizards as part of a religious ritual.

Other criminal offences were punished by a fine called 'wergild', a part of which was paid to the state and part to the victim or his kin. Murder, wounding and theft were avenged by either the victim, where possible, or his kin. It was therefore desirable to have a large number of kin who could exact vengeance on an offender. It was known that retribution from a victim or his kin would be more swift and certain than that from a remote and disinterested body such as the state.

Compensation and retribution were allowed only to those of the rank of freeman or above. Most slaves, or bondsmen, were probably captives or debtors. In those places where communities held land in common, bondsmen were presumably owned jointly and put to work on tasks which benefited the community as a whole. When, and where, there was greater private ownership, they are more likely to have been owned by individual people. Where the latter case applied it is probable that some performed household duties but most were like tenants who in return for rendering services to their owners were provided with a house and land. Payment may have been set at a given amount of grain, livestock, cloth or other produce each year or it may have taken the form of an obligation to provide a certain number of days labour at ploughing, sowing and harvest times. Bondsmen could not carry arms or participate in the political life of the community. If a slave was killed, compensation was paid to his owner and not to his family who had no right of retribution.

The moot elected a law officer and one hundred respected advisers for the settlement of civil disputes. The law officer visited settlements at regular intervals to hear disputes and make judgements. Some of the one hundred advisers accompanied him to the hearings and lent weight to his decisions. They probably also acted as witnesses to the proper conduct of the proceedings, the verdict reached, the compensation awarded and the punishment given. Perhaps just twelve of the advisers were employed on such duties at any one time. Such a system may have been a forerunner of the jury system.

When a young man was competent in the use of weapons and had reached a given age he attended a moot and was presented with a spear and shield by his leader, or his father, or one of his kin. Only warriors were allowed to carry arms and all business, public or private, was conducted with both parties armed. The presentation of the spear and shield therefore had a civil as well as a military significance as it marked the acceptance of the young man as a freeman and a warrior.

If the moot decided on a course of military action, all freemen were duty bound to fight for their community. However not all armed conflict was between nations. A lord might put forward plans, at the moot, for a venture of his own. He could call on the warriors for support and those who gave it were bound to join his following for the undertaking he had put forward. Warlords led their followers on raids into enemy territory or they fought as mercenaries. Young warriors joined such ventures in order to prove their worth, both to themselves and others, and to find fame.

Warfare and Runes

The Germanic peoples used symbols called runes to represent the mysterious forces of nature, the blessing of life, and the curse of death. Runes were used for magical purposes but they became increasingly important as a form of writing. As the language and the requirements of those skilled in magic changed and evolved so new runes were devised and old ones modified to suit the new needs. Sometimes the rune-masters created new runes by merging existing ones or they borrowed and adapted signs from the peoples of the south. Whatever the origin of individual runes, and however great or few their number, they continued to be used for magic, divination and writing.

The pieces of wood on which the runes were engraved were called 'runakeffle', (runic key). Runes were a way of communicating with the Gods and the Sisters Wyrd, and the piece of wood on which they were cut was a key to the mysteries of Wyrd and all the worlds of creation.

Runes were also marked on swords to denote the maker or owner, and victory-runes invoked Tiw the god of courage and glory. Runic charms were sometimes marked on possessions to protect them from theft, and craftsmen inscribed them on pieces of bone, wood or other material that they were about to work, in order to guard against mistakes or prevent breakage.

Women were recognized as having greater powers of prophecy than men, and the fame of some seeresses was widespread and their power and influence very great. Such women were called *Alrynia* and were skilled in the use of runes and the casting of lots. They and their followers were accorded privileges and high status when they visited those who sought their services. Alrynia were often consulted before wars and other enterprises were undertaken.

Many decisions were taken by the casting of lots. The fate of enemy prisoners was sometimes determined in this way and it is recorded that lots were cast on three successive days to decide whether a captive should be killed by fire, and on each occasion it was decreed that he should live. Important leadership decisions were sometimes taken in the same way. The Continental, or Old Saxons, continued at a late date to be ruled by regional kings who, when war threatened, met to decide by the casting of lots which of them should lead the whole Saxon nation for the duration of the conflict.

Battlefield tactics were sometimes determined by lots. When Ariovist, the leader of the Sueb was confronted by a Roman army he followed the customary procedure and let the matrons of the tribe decide by means of lots and divinations when it would be most advantageous to attack the enemy.

One of the early procedures for the casting of lots was to cut a branch from a nut-bearing tree and split the wood into strips. Symbols were marked on the pieces of wood which were then thrown on to a white cloth. A prayer was offered to the Gods by the person conducting the ceremony and then, with eyes looking to the sky, three strips were picked up, one at a time, and their meaning read out. If the signs were unfavourable, the matter was put off to another day. If the signs were good a favourable omen might be sought from the observation of the flight and song of birds, or from the movements and noises of sacred horses which were kept for that special purpose. In the latter case a wizard and the leader of the council of elders, or the king, hitched the horses to a sacred wagon and then walked beside them listening to their snorts and neighs. If the matter being considered was war, and the omens for battle were good, the wizards brought emblems from the sacred grove and prepared them for carriage into battle. A ceremony was held in which the assistance of the gods was sought and the leader might pledge all the spoils of war to Tiw and Woden in return for success in battle. A special spear was prepared and marked with the runes of victory. The enemy was promised as a sacrifice to the gods and before the battle began a chosen warrior hurled the spear over the heads of the enemy in order to seal the bargain.

In the event of a victory all the weapons and war-coats of the foe were bent and broken and thrown into a lake or bog and their bodies hung from trees. The sacrifice was great as much of the war-gear consisted of swords, helmets and war-coats which were of great value. When a Germanic tribe, the Cimbre, defeated a large Roman army in 105 BC they captured a huge amount of equipment and valuables. Orosius tells how the Romans and all their possessions were destroyed in order to honour a pledge that in return for being granted victory the enemy would be sacrificed to the gods. All clothing was ripped to pieces; gold and silver was flung into the river; the war-coats were hacked to pieces; horses drowned and their harnesses destroyed, prisoners hung from the trees by their necks, and nothing was left for the victors and no mercy shown to the defeated.

Tacitus records that in AD 58 two German tribes, the Chatti and the Hermunduri, fought a great battle over possession of a rich salt-producing river. Each side dedicated the other to Tiw and Woden and when the Chatti were defeated all survivors, equipment and horses were destroyed.

Funerals

The wardens of the Old Ways conducted funeral rites and supervised the construction of funeral pyres. Usually only one body was burnt on each pyre but after a battle the victors collected the bodies of their dead comrades and placed them together on the bed of wood. The weapons of the dead warriors were thrown into the fire and sometimes the bodies of their horses were burnt with them. Special timbers were used for the pyres of great people, and their remains were buried under mounds of earth, the size and location of which depended upon their status.

The mourners ate seeds which symbolized rebirth, and handfuls of grain, herbs and potions were thrown into the flames. The act of burning released the soul from the body and allowed it to rise with the heat and smoke into Heaven. The ceremony was simple and although women were able to express their grief men were not expected to do so other than in their words of praise for the dead. For some it was the custom to place the ashes of the dead in patterned clay pots which were sometimes marked with runes and buried in shallow graves. Personal possessions of the dead were often placed in the grave which was marked only by a raised mound of turf. In those places where it was the custom to bury bodies in the ground, the rites accompanying the burials were similar to those used at cremations. For example grain was burned in a dish and then placed in the grave.

Evidence from later English cemeteries shows that fires were sometimes lit in the grave, perhaps to harden or purify the soil, before the unburnt body was placed in it. Burials were sometimes sprinkled with charcoal which may have been the remains of a fire lit next to the grave as part of the burial ritual. When wooden coffins were used the surface of them was sometimes burned before the body was placed in them. The purpose of this practice may have been to harden the wood to help preserve it but the process of burning it would probably have formed part of the ritual. Large pieces of burned timber were sometimes placed beside the coffin and may have had the same symbolic meaning as the Yule log which represented continuity. Small fire pits were made near the graves, presumably for use during the ceremony and may have been used to burn personal possessions of the deceased. Personal items placed in the grave were often broken or damaged in some way perhaps as a symbolic gesture to end their life, or possibly to deter grave robbers or to symbolize a spiritual break with the deceased and discourage their recovery and use for magical purposes. When the grave was closed large stones were sometimes placed on the grave, perhaps as a memorial or, as has been suggested, to prevent the body rising from the grave. If such was the case the practice probably had connections with magical beliefs. A more practical explanation for the stones is that they prevented animals digging up the corpse.

Much of the ritual accompanying internments seems to have been carried over from cremation ceremonies. For example the custom of throwing corn on to the funeral pyre probably gave rise to the practice of burning corn in a dish and placing it in the grave. Latter inhumations/internments sometimes contained joints of meat and may have represented the deceased person's share of a last meal, which was perhaps cooked and eaten at the graveside.

The usual explanation given for the placing of items in a grave is that they were for use in the next life. This seems to be the stock answer but there is no evidence to suggest that that was the purpose of the deposits and there is little to suggest that the heathen English believed in a life after death. The indications are that they believed this to be the only life and that as a result it was to be lived to the full. Death seems to have been regarded as a curse, the fact of which was to be used, if possible, as a means of enhancing one's fame which would live on in the minds of those left behind. For the very famous, heroic deeds were recorded in verse and became part of the culture and mythology of that, and other societies.

The Engle

In the fourth century C.E. in lands from the Elbe to the fjords of northern Jutland, there lived seven tribes who were united in their worship of Mother Earth. One of those peoples was the Engle and their country was called Angeln. Nerthus was the name by which they called the Earth Mother and her presence was symbolized by an idol which was kept in a covered waggon, in a small wood, on an island in the sea. It was covered with a cloth and cared for by the wardens of the Old Ways. When the time was right the waggon, accompanied by a wizard, was drawn by cows from settlement to settlement and everywhere it went there followed days of celebration and merry-making. During the travels all iron objects were locked away and no one took up arms or went to war. When the travels were ended the wizard returned the waggon to its holy place where it and its contents were washed in a secret lake by slaves who were drowned when the cleansing had been completed.

The chief place of worship for each of these tribes was situated near the middle of their territory. They followed the example of the Gods and made their places of congregation and worship by lakes, springs and pools. In some places wooden idols were placed on piles of stones in the middle of bogs and tall poles were also set up, either singly or in groups. Sacrificial items were placed in the waters around the idols, and the gifts reflected what was being sought from the gods, and the importance of the place of worship. At first sacrifices were mostly animals, household items and agricultural tools, but, later, manufactured ornaments, clothing, wooden vessels, war-gear and even ships, were placed in the bogs.

The ritual slaughter of animals was carried out by a wizard who killed most of the animals with a blow to their forehead. The head, feet, tail and skin of each animal were removed and prepared for burial. Sometimes the severed parts were placed in the earth together, at other times apart. They might be buried in the earthen floor of a newly built house or be put into the waters of a sacred pool or bog. The entrails were sometimes placed in pots and left at a shrine, while the flesh was cooked and served at a feast held in honour of the God to whom the sacrifice had been made.

Most of the sacrificed animals were ordinary farm animals but some were horses or dogs. The sacrifice of a horse was a great loss as they were not only expensive animals which conferred status on their owners but were also considered sacred. Horse-gear, such as bridles, saddles and spurs, was sometimes thrown into a bog as a sacrifice, or buried with the remains of its owner. Dogs were not eaten, but were killed on the death of their master and buried with his remains.

Sometimes warriors drew lots before battle for the purpose of deciding which one of their number was to be sacrificed to Woden but most human sacrifices were of criminals who had already been sentenced to death. They were taken to a holy place where they might be stripped, bound and blindfolded before having a woollen thread tied round one of their ankles. Then, at the appropriate stage in the ritual, the victim was hanged with a hide noose, or strangled with a cord or hazel branch. The feet, the hands, or the head were sometimes removed from the corpse and buried separately before the remains were put into a bog or pool. Sodomites and oath-breakers were bound and pushed face down into the waters under a wicker hurdle, or under branches, which were weighed down with stones.

As the influence and power of warriors in society became greater so the number, and extent, of the sacrifices to the war gods increased, but many sacrifices were still made to Thunor and the gods and goddesses of fertility and the sea. Wooden idols with clearly defined male and female sexual parts were cast into the pools and bogs as part of a ritual to invoke the favour of the gods, and some fertility idols were stood upright in the bogs. Male fertility figures, sometimes ten feet high, were more common and generally much larger than the female figures. In areas where there were no bogs, the people dug pits and shafts, and the sacrifices, some in pots, were placed in them. The holes were refilled and sometimes a pile of stones was placed over them.

The waters of the North Sea were abundant with fish. The people living at the edge of the ocean took much of their food from it and, in recognition of its importance to them, a shrine dedicated to Nehalennia, a goddess of the sea's fertility, was established on an island off the coast. Sea-fishing helped the people to become expert boat builders and sailors, and those skills were made use of by warlords who sought adventure and fame, on land and at sea. At first the war bands raided nearby coastal and river settlements, but as their skills and the need for new targets increased, so they sailed greater distances, sometimes reaching the coast of Spain. Before setting out the warriors sought a safe passage from the gods and goddesses of the sea, and from the giants and giantesses who lived in it. They asked for favourable winds and currents, and vowed that in exchange for a safe journey they would cast gifts to the mighty spear-man that is the sea. A letter written by Sidonius, about the year 470, reveals the form those gifts may have taken. He described how the Saxons after raiding the lands to the south performed a rite on the eve of their setting sail. By the casting of lots one tenth of the prisoners they had with them were selected for sacrifice by crucifixion or drowning.

Offa King of the Engle

In the time before the English came to Britain they lived in the land between the seas north of the river Eider. They were known as the Engle and their country was called Angeln. In the 4th century Wermund, son of Wihtlaeg, was their king and his domain stretched from the Baltic coast in the east to the North Sea coast in the west. To the north were the Jutes and beyond the river Eider to the south were the Myrgings and Saxons.

Wermund wed the daughter of his oldest and most trusted companion Freawine and she gave him his only son Offa. The boy was sent, as was the custom, to live in the household of one of the king's companions. Freawine had been appointed by Wermund to govern Slesvig, the southern district of his kingdom, and it was to him that the honour of preparing Offa for manhood and kingship was given. Freawine had two sons of his own, Keto and Wiga, who, although much older than Offa, became his close companions. They, and their chief warrior Falco, helped train him in the ways and arts of war and prepared him for his initiation as a warrior. Offa, being gifted with a powerful body, sharp wits and quick reflexes, became a formidable swordsman and was well liked by all who knew him.

When Offa was thirteen, Eadgils, lord of the Myrgings, landed with a large force and surrounded Freawine's hall. Eadgils sent a messenger to inform Freawine that he had come to demand tribute and that if Freawine refused to pay he could either fight Eadgils in single combat or face a bloody battle in which everyone in the hall was certain to die. Freawine agreed to fight, and was killed by Eadgils who announced that he would return later to collect his tribute.

31

Wermund, upon hearing of Freawine's death, appointed Keto and Wiga as joint rulers in his place. The brothers set about preparing for the return of Eadgils and although Offa stayed with them it was arranged that he should be sent to a place of safety before the king of the Myrgings returned. However the king outwitted them and, reappearing earlier than expected, he surrounded their enclosure, and demanded the tribute due to him. He also demanded that the Engle evacuate the northern bank of the Eider so as to remove any threat they might pose to the Myrgings. The brothers refused to yield to the demand and gave Falco the task of escaping, at night, through the enemy lines to tell Wermund of their plight. Falco managed to reach the king, who was at Jællinge, and in gratitude for his bravery Wermund presented Falco with a golden cup and provided him with a host of warriors. Falco swore that he would, if necessary, fight to the death in defence of Offa and Angeln, and said that if Wyrd gave him victory he would drink as much blood as the cup would hold. The blood would be either his own or that of Eadgils.

Falco went quickly south with the warriors and confronted Eadgils who was still laying siege to the hall in which the companions were sheltering. After a ferocious battle the Myrgings were forced to flee to their ships and despite the bravery of Falco, Eadgils escaped. Falco was true to his oath and as he stood on the shore watching Eadgils's ships sail into the distance he opened a wound received in the fighting and trickled blood into his helmet and drank from it.

Keto and Wiga hatched a plan to avenge the death of their father. They left Falco in charge of the district and, disguised as Frisian merchants, they set sail for the land of the Myrgings. Late in the voyage they discovered Offa hidden among the cargo but, as the winds were favourable, they sailed on and soon arrived in the domain of Eadgils. They were taken with a sample of their wares to the king's hall where they were shown in to see him. After inspecting the goods, Eadgils offered them his hospitality, and after a meal they were provided with lodgings. During the following few days samples of the ship's cargo were transported to the king's hall and much of it was to his liking. He was particularly interested in a very fine pattern-welded sword. After several days the threesome gained the confidence of Eadgils and were entertained by him alone at night in the high hall, drinking, playing dice and talking. When it was late, and after Eadgils had sampled a large amount of wine, Keto revealed his true identity and challenged Eadgils to fight. The king readily agreed and weapons were selected from among those the brothers had brought with them. Despite the vast amount Eadgils had drunk, he still had the beating of his challenger and Keto was forced into a corner. Wiga, fearing for his brother's life, grabbed a torch from its stand and crashed it down on the kings head. For a moment he was stunned and in that instant Keto killed him.

When the infamous deed had been done Keto and Wiga grabbed Offa and made their way quietly to the three prepared horses tethered nearby and rode through the moonlit countryside to their ship. As soon as Offa and the brothers were aboard, the ship pulled away from the shore and, assisted by the current, its oars propelled the boat down the river to the flat silver sea.

The brothers arrived back in Angeln and told how Keto had, with skill and courage, fought and killed Eadgils to avenge his father's death. On the strength of that tale Wermundus and all the people welcomed them as heroes. However a different story was put about by the kindred of Eadgils and soon it reached Angeln. It was not one of bravery but of treachery and cowardice. The Engle sensed the truth of this account and, being an honourable people, they regarded the matter as a national disgrace.

From the day of the killing Offa didn't speak a word and could not be induced to confirm or deny the story told by his companions. Offa was bound by bonds of loyalty to them and could not deny their account of events, but honour prevented him from confirming it. He decided to pay a penance of silence for the cowardly deed.

Offa's friendship with Keto and Wiga faded and he became solitary and withdrawn. Within a year or two he was regarded as dull and foolish, and his early promise as a warrior was soon forgotten, though he remained very strong. Much of his time was spent in the company of a wizard who taught him many skills.

Many years later when Wermundus was old and very poor of sight, a messenger came to him from the king of the Myrgings demanding that he surrender his kingdom or fight for it in single combat. If the king wished, and he had a son capable, the matter could be decided by the sons of the two kings fighting in single combat. Wermundus despite his years still had fire in him and he was angered by the challenge. The king decided it would be better for him to die with honour in combat than surrender or see his stupid son butchered.

Offa was in his thirtieth year and had not spoken since his trip to Saxony but on hearing of the challenge he said that he would not only fight the son of the king of Saxony but also his champion. Offa hoped that the combat, however it went, would wipe out the disgrace that had been brought on the Engle by Keto and Wiga.

It was agreed that the combat would take place at Rendsburg on an island in the Eider. The river separated the two kingdoms. A date was set and Offa set about obtaining armour and a sword suited to his great strength. During all but one of the few days available he practised his fighting skills. On his rest day he visited the wizard and there he travelled out of this world to a place where his mind was made firm and his belief in victory made absolute. Before he left his old friend, the wizard scratched the rune of Tiw on Offa's sword and gave him a charm to carry with him.

Offa travelled to Rendsburg and on the appointed day he went to the place of combat. All those who saw him were impressed by his sense of purpose and destiny. However, Wermundus was so certain that his son would be slain by his well-practised opponents that at the time of the combat he stood on a high bridge ready, on receipt of news of his son's death, to throw himself into the torrent below.

Offa first killed the Saxon king's champion, then the son and in doing so won single-handedly land to the south of the Eider for his father and gained everlasting fame. Upon the death of Wermundus, Offa became king of a great domain.

Offa and Drida

A small boat without sail or oar was washed on to the beach. Lying in the boat in an exhausted state was a young woman who had spent many nights at sea. The clothing she wore indicated that she was from a wealthy, high-ranking, family. She was taken to the king's hall where she rested for several days. When she had recovered she revealed that her name was Drida, and that she had been cast adrift because she had refused an offer of marriage. The real reason for her punishment was that she had murdered her young brother but, because she was related to the king, she had been cast adrift instead of being put to death.

Offa provided Drida with a fine place to live and everything she required. After several months, and despite the warnings of some of his kin who suspected she was not all that she seemed, Offa and Drida were married. Her name was changed to Quendrida and she and Offa had three daughters. Quendrida did her utmost to persuade Offa to have them married to Frankish princes but Offa preferred to find them husbands elsewhere and as a result the two elder daughters were given in marriage to kings who were his allies. The third daughter, named Aelfleda, who was much like her mother in looks and temperament, was to be married to King Aethelberht. Quendrida did all she could to persuade Offa that Aethelberht was unworthy of their daughter but without success. The Queen desperately wanted a Frankish alliance for the purpose of enabling her to return to her homeland. She took her daughter into her confidence and explained her plan to gain a Frankish alliance and to use it to destroy Offa and make herself, and Aelfleda, the most powerful force in the land. Together they hatched a plot to kill Aethelberht and bring dishonour on Offa.

When Aethelberht visited Offa the pair sat together each evening with several companions and an old wizard whom Offa had known from childhood. Quendrida entered the hall and sat by King Aethelberht. She discreetly told him that her daughter wished to see him in her chamber but that he should be careful not to be seen going there. When the opportunity arose the young king made his way unseen to Aelfleda's room. When he entered she beckoned him to sit on a chair which had been placed on a trapdoor in the floor. Shortly after Aethelberht had sat down the door opened and he fell down a shaft into a secret passage where he was murdered by the Queen's loyal servant.

The disappearance of Aethelberht presented great difficulties for Offa who, after a long search, was unable to find an explanation for the disappearance of his guest. Offa decided to travel with the dead king's companions to Aethelberht's hall to give news of the mysterious disappearance. Before the party set out, the wizard discovered the passage beneath the chamber and found the body of Aethelberht buried there. He revealed the find to Aethelberht's close friend and told him how he believed the deed had been done and how the death could be avenged. When the party set out for the homeward journey the friend slipped away on the first night and returned to Offa's hall where he killed Offa's wife and daughter, and, with the help of the wizard, buried their bodies in the passage next to that of the dead king. The next day the wizard had the passage filled in and the bodies were never found. Aethelberht's kin heard from his companion about the fate of the king and his murderers, and being content that justice had been done, and that Offa was entirely innocent, they parted company with Offa on good terms and peace prevailed.

The Beginning of a New Age

By the end of the fourth century the Germanic tribes were spread far and wide across northern Europe. Their societies had developed in different ways, and they often fought each other, but they were aware of their common roots and identity. The migrations and wars of that time resulted in the break-up of some tribal alliances and the creation of others, with the result that new loyalties and new elites were formed. For example, at the end of the first century C.E. there is no record of the Saxons and Franks but by the fifth century they were two of the most powerful confederations of people in Northern Europe.

The early 5th century was a time of great importance for the Germanic tribes who had by that time taken control of nearly all the territory on the east bank of the Rhine and held most of the north bank of the Danube. There had been several military successes against the Romans in the east but in the west there had been no recent breakthrough. Those who crossed the Rhine into Gaul usually did so for the purpose of seizing movable wealth but a new wave of migration, and invasion from the east, created the need for new land to settle. It became apparent that some degree of co-operation between the tribes would be necessary if a major defeat were to be inflicted on the Romans. Such an alliance came into being in 406 when a force of Vandals, Swabians, Burgundians and Alans gathered on the east bank of the Rhine. It is probable that omens were sought, runes read and lots cast before they launched their attack across that powerful river. They fought their way through the enemy defences and broke them so that when the fighting was done they had the whole of Gaul before them. In an attempt to re-establish control the Romans withdrew troops from Britain but they were unable to recover their position in Gaul.

During the breakthrough the Asding king Godegisel was killed but his son took command and led the Vandals into Gaul and then into Spain. In 429 they crossed to North Africa and captured Carthage and forced the Romans to formally cede a large part of that territory to them. The Vandals then landed in Sicily and forced further concessions from the Romans. After a period of peace a new wave of activity started around the year 455 with the capture of Corsica, Sardinia and the Balearic Islands. Raids were made on the coast of Spain and Greece, and a landing in Italy culminated in the capture and sacking of Rome.

The Swabians, like the Vandals, moved across Gaul to the Iberian peninsula where they established their own kingdom. The Burgundians remained in the east of Gaul and eventually created a kingdom which had two capitals; one at Lyons and the other at Geneva. The Alans went to Spain and North Africa but gradually lost their identity and became merged with the Vandals who in turn became absorbed into the populations of the conquered territories.

The Alamans and Franks made less spectacular advances into Gaul than the Vandals and other tribes but their gains were to be more long-lasting as they captured and settled land lying next to their existing territory. The Alamans, which means 'all men', were a confederation of several Germanic peoples, the largest group being Swabians.

The Franks were also a mixture, or confederation, of peoples who lived near the Rhine. They did not take part in the events of 406 but were able to take advantage of the disintegration of Roman power in northern Gaul and move into territory adjacent to their own. Their advance was mostly by means of steady migration rather than sweeping military conquest. Towards the end of the 5th century the Franks became a powerful people and much later one of their kings, Charles the Great (Charlemagne) 742-814, went on to create a great empire. The Frankish population was, however, quite small compared with that living in the Empire they created, and although they gave their name, and much else, to France, their separate identity was eventually lost in the large Gallic population.

The victory of 406 CE dealt a great blow to the Roman position in Gaul and to the Empire as a whole and was one from which it never recovered. In the east the Goths moved into Italy and took Rome in 410, and in the extreme west the seaborne expansion of the North Sea tribes (Saxons) contributed to the Roman abandonment of Britain. The success of the various Germanic tribes in following up the victory depended mainly on the size of their population and the extent of the new territory they controlled. The Vandals travelled great distances, and made a powerful impact, before disappearing almost without trace. The Franks moved into territory adjoining their own and created a kingdom that was to grow into a powerful empire. It can be seen that in the struggle for survival between peoples, conflict and conquest can take the following forms:

1. raids into enemy territory for the purpose of obtaining treasure;
2. invasions in which the enemy are defeated militarily and made a subject people who pay tribute to their conquerors who remain in their own country;
3. invasion and conquest by a comparatively small group who take up residence and form a ruling military elite;
4. invasion and defeat of the enemy followed by tribal migration and displacement of the earlier population.

The fourth form of invasion is the only one to bring lasting results. A people who remain on the land, and are more numerous than the invaders, can survive many defeats and long periods of foreign rule. Elites can be overthrown or be absorbed into the native population.

The Saxons and Frisians

The feelings of empathy and loyalty that bind people together and help them to perceive themselves as being separate and distinct from their neighbours varies from time to time and place to place. The Saxons were a mixture of peoples united by a family of warrior kings while the unity of the Frisians was based primarily on their long history and comparative isolation. The unity of the Engle was in part based on

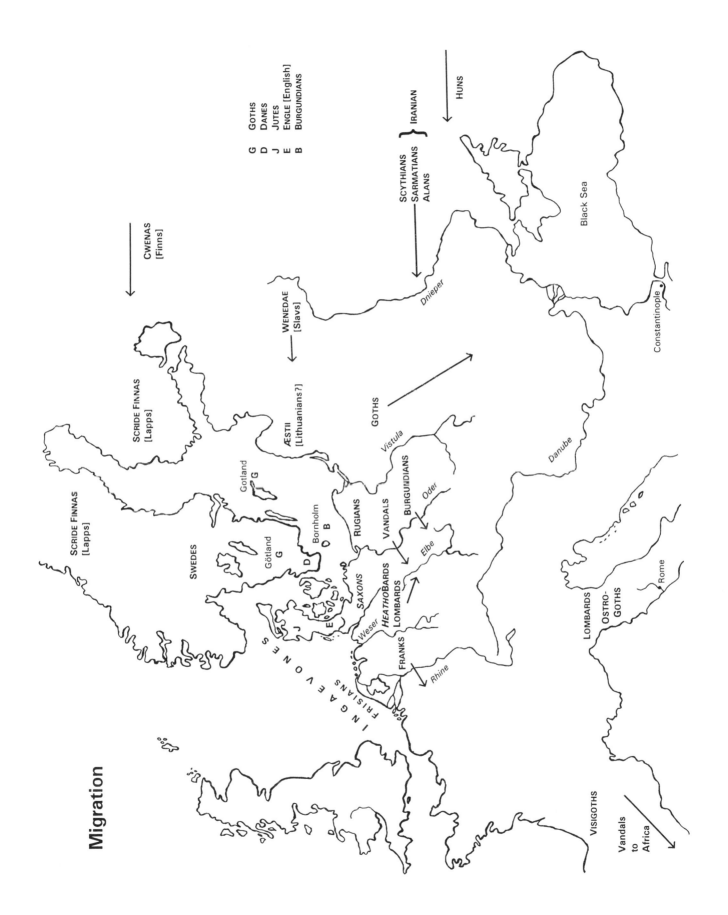

Migration

SCRIDE FINNAS [Lapps]

SCRIDE FINNAS [Lapps]

CWENAS [Finns]

SWEDES

Gotland G

Götland G

Bornholm B

D

WENEDAE [Slavs]

ÆSTII [Lithuanians?]

SAXONS

RUGIANS

E

J

INGAEVONES

FRISIANS

Weser

HEATHOBARDS

LOMBARDS

VANDALS

BURGUNDIANS

FRANKS

Rhine

Elbe

Oder

Vistula

GOTHS

SCYTHIANS
SARMATIANS
ALANS } IRANIAN

Dnieper

HUNS

Black Sea

Constantinople

Danube

LOMBARDS

OSTRO-
GOTHS

Rome

VISIGOTHS

Vandals
to
Africa

G   GOTHS
D   DANES
J   JUTES
E   ENGLE [English]
B   BURGUNDIANS

common religious practices. All of these tribes had contact with Britain; the Frisians primarily as traders, the Saxons and the Engle as raiders and mercenaries.

The Saxons were a confederation of peoples who lived in the lands between the lower Rhine and Jutland. When under external threat they were united by a family of warrior kings but their political unity in times of peace was not very great and many warlords took independent military action. The Saxons were as feared at sea as on land. Their ships were well-designed and well-built, and it was recorded by a Roman writer that their courage was so great and their seamanship so expert that they welcomed a storm because of the opportunity it gave them to take their enemy by surprise. Their attacks on the coasts of Gaul and Britain, and on Roman, Gallic and British ships, became so frequent and troublesome that the Romans tried to sweep the Saxons from the sea. Despite the considerable resources devoted to the task they were unsuccessful and the attacks continued. The Romans also built strongholds at strategic points on those parts of the coast of Britain and Gaul known as the Saxon Shore.

After the victory of the Germanic tribes in 406 and the withdrawal of Roman forces from Britain, the Saxon war bands increased the frequency and duration of their raids which in 408 were on such a large scale that they amounted to an invasion. The British leaders appealed to the Romans for help but none was given. It is probable that most of the North Sea tribes took part in the raids but they became known collectively, by foreigners, after the name of the largest and probably most active group of raiders, the Saxons.

The Frisians were among the first of the North Sea peoples to cross to Britain and settle there. They went as traders and farmers, and settled in the east of Britain in the sparsely populated areas between the Thames and The Wash. Frisian merchants traded with the Britons and some went to live in the ports and other towns of eastern Britain where they were able to acquire information about the happenings in that land. The merchants' knowledge of Britain and their trade routes across the North Sea resulted in them becoming increasingly involved in the movement of settlers and their belongings to Britain. Frisian cargo ships were better suited than Saxon or Engle warships to the task of carrying baggage and cattle. The early Frisian involvement in seaborne trade and settlement led to their language becoming known beyond their own land and Frisian played a part in the development of the English language, to which it is closely related. North of the Frisians and Saxons, across the Eider, were the Engle who, as we have seen, were united in their worship of Nerthus. They were a considerable military force but they may have been, in the main, a Baltic sea-power. To the north of them were the Eote (Jutes).

Britain

It is evident from history that those with the greatest power take the best land while the weak have to be content with poorer soils. In the distant past Britain was inhabited by a people we call the Ivernians or Hibernians, most of whom lived on the fertile and easily cultivated lands of the south and east. They were driven off that land by invading Gaels (Goidels) a Celtic people who came to Britain from the continent. The Gaels were better armed and organized than the Hibernians, many of whom moved to high ground or into the forests that covered much of Britain. The Gaels were greatly influenced by Druidism, the religion of the Ivernians, and some of them adapted and developed it for their own purposes.

After the Gaels came the Britons (Brythons) another Celtic people who in turn drove out many Gaels and took the best districts. As Gaels migrated to the north and west, they conquered, or pushed before them, the Ivernians and Hibernians who were only able to be free in Ireland and the north of Britain. The power of the Britons increased and their control of much of the island that was to be given their name became firmer. As it did so the Gaels moved further north and west. Many Gaels went to Ireland where they occupied the eastern districts while the Ivernians and Hibernians lived in the west. In those parts of western Britain where the two peoples had to live together the population became mixed and it was only in the north of Britain and the west of Ireland that the Ivernians and Hibernians were able to preserve their identity.

Tribes of Belgic Gauls crossed the sea to Britain during the period of German and Roman expansion and there were also migrations of non-Celtic people. The most unusual journey was made by some North African Berbers who arrived in Spain and then sailed to the west coast of Britain where they settled and created a kingdom on the western shore of what is now Wales.

In the north of Britain there lived tribes to whom the Romans gave the collective name Caledonians. The most powerful of those people were the Picts. Little is known about them but it has been suggested that they may have been either one of the earliest tribes to migrate to Britain, having entered from the south, or possibly one of Germanic origin and to have migrated from Norway via the Shetland Islands.

Many people of that time painted their bodies when they went to war but the Picts seem to have developed the custom more than most and had permanent tattoos of a unique style. They also used a distinctive form of writing, and patterns, both of which they engraved on rocks.

The population of Britain consisted of an assortment of ethnic groups who, as far as possible, sought to control their own territory and defended it in a collective way. Sometimes the incoming population was comparatively small in number and formed a military elite that ruled over a long established population. During the great periods of European migration the number of persons on the move, and seeking land on which to settle, was very great. A people, or tribe, might number one hundred thousand individuals or more. The effect of one or more such groups on the move was widespread disturbance and conflict. Some tribes were powerful enough to resist such pressures and to hold their territory but others were driven from their land and sought more elsewhere. It was the custom at that time for individuals to migrate as part of a large group as it made them stronger in defence and attack, and enabled them to retain their cultural identity.

As we have seen, it was the custom of the Germanic peoples to sacrifice captives to the gods but sometimes prisoners were taken, either to ransom or to keep as slaves. Presumably any skills the slaves had were made use of but many were probably put to work as labourers. The extent to which slaves were absorbed into the societies they served is not known but much probably depended upon the extent to which they were physically and culturally similar to their captors. Slaves that were surplus to requirements were often sold to traders and transported to Roman slave markets where demand was high. It is possible that many of the earthworks found in Britain and Europe were built shortly after wars when there was an abundance of slave labour, or perhaps they were the result of communal organization and effort.

The English and Welsh

The people of the North Sea tribes (Jutes, Frisians, Saxons and Engle) were known to the people of Britain as Saxons, but when they settled in Britain their country came to be called England, and their language, English. These North Sea migrants will hereafter be referred to as being English or Anglo-Saxon.

The non-English population of what is now England and Wales were known to the English as 'Welsh' (O.E. *wealh*, meaning foreigner or slave). In reality, as we have seen, the Welsh were a mixture of peoples, many of whom had adopted various aspects of Celtic culture, especially language, although it is unlikely that many of them were ethnic Celts. In order to simplify matters this population will be referred to as the Welsh, and the inhabitants of Ireland will be called Gaels. The homeland of the Picts was known to the English as Pictland and roughly corresponded with what is now Scotland.

Roman Britain

When the Romans conquered Britain they did so for the purpose of absorbing it into their empire and governing the people, not settling the land. Many of the troops used in the conquest and later defence of Britain were Germanic and their camps were usually in strategic defensive positions either close to, or inside, Roman fortifications. The Roman forts at Brancaster, Burgh, Bradwell, Reculver, Richborough, Dover, Lympne, Pevensey and Portchester were strategic strong points in the Saxon Shore defences which stretched from The Wash to the Isle of Wight. Norwich and York were important garrison towns and there were German camps guarding the lower Thames (Mucking) and the southern approaches to London (Croydon and Mitcham). Germanic mercenaries were also stationed along the Middle Thames to provide protection for the heartland of southern Britain.

Some of the warriors serving as Roman mercenaries stayed on in Britain after their term of service ended, and continued to live in or near the settlements that had grown up by the camps and were able to obtain there the goods and services that were being provided locally for the garrisons. They were able to enjoy contact with other Germans and also the security that such settlements offered. It was in this way that small Germanic communities were created in Britain even before the Romans abandoned it in 410. Many of those communities survived the economic upheaval of the Roman withdrawal and were strengthened by the arrival of settlers seeking new land. The reason for the movement of people from North West Europe to Britain was in part due to the rising sea levels that occurred at that time and the resulting flooding and salt contamination of low lying arable land along sea coasts and river mouths.

When the Romans abandoned Britain, those Welsh who had benefited from the Roman occupation naturally wished to preserve Roman customs and forms of administration. They had grown accustomed to living in towns and wanted to maintain the economic and political system that made the Roman way of life possible. They believed the Roman withdrawal was only temporary and that once the legions had re-established the boundaries of the empire on the Continent they would return to Britain and restore the position of their allies and the Church. Their response to Saxon and Pictish raids was to appeal to the Romans for help rather than to attempt to unite and provide for their own defence.

After the Roman withdrawal the political and economic structures they had created started to decay, as did the towns, churches and estates that were a part of that society. The partially suppressed culture and way of life of the Welsh was able to re-emerge, as were the ancient hostilities. As is common when an imperial power declines, there was a struggle for power between tribes, and various local leaders and factions fought each other for political control.

The Welsh managed to unite for the purpose of repelling an invasion of Picts in 410 but following that the struggle for power continued. After many years a Welsh king named Votigern achieved a position of dominance and became overlord. The Welsh continued to fight amongst themselves and while they did so Engle, Frisians, and Saxons crossed the sea to Britain and steadily strengthened their position in the East. The lack of unity among the Welsh may indicate that tribal and ethnic divisions were greater than is now sometimes thought.

The twenty years following the Roman withdrawal were not all ones of war and there were times of peace and prosperity but that comparatively tranquil period came to an end about the year 430 with an outbreak of plague and renewed Pictish attacks. After suffering several defeats at the hands of the Picts, the Welsh decided to seek help from abroad. There were still some of them who wished to re-introduce Roman power but Vortigern was opposed to that policy, probably because he thought it would undermine his own position, and decided to recruit mercenaries to fight against the Picts. The natural thing to do was to employ the warriors that the Romans had used. Vortigern sent a messenger across the sea with an appeal for help.

Hengest and Horsa

A messenger from Vortigern arrived at the hall of Hengest and his twin brother Horsa. They were invited to Britain with their companions to protect the Welsh and drive out the Picts, and as a reward for entering into the service of Vortigern, they were promised land and provisions. The offer was accepted and a host of warriors set sail in three longships and landed at a place called Ypwinesfleot (Ebbsfleet, Kent). They took possession of the land that had been given them (Isle of Thanet) and then went north in their ships to fight the Picts who had been attacking the Welsh on land and from the sea. Hengest and Horsa were victorious wherever they went and drove out the Picts and brought peace to the land.

The warriors served Vortigern well for many years and there was peace and prosperity in Britain and each year they received the food, and other provisions that had been promised them as payment for their services. Their success, and the economic and political stability it helped bring, encouraged more of their fellow countrymen to cross the sea and their number in the east of Britain increased, and as it did so the Welsh gradually abandoned much of that area and migrated westwards. The need for people to live with those of their own kind is very strong and the Welsh preferred to withdraw and seek new land rather than live in areas that were being increasingly populated by people who could not be, and had no wish to be, absorbed into their society and culture. In those early years of settlement the English gained control of territory in the east by a gradual and steady increase in their numbers rather than by force of arms. The taking of land by one people from another is more often achieved by migration than military conquest. When the process is gradual, and the will to organize and resist it is absent, the point eventually comes when the newcomers have control of the land. The people whose country it is are sometimes driven to fight to defend their territory and their independence but often nothing is done until the position is hopeless. Each person expects another to act and unless a leader emerges nothing effective is done. More often the people drift away to another part of their country and abandon increasingly large parts of it to the newcomers.

Shortly after 440, following a long period of peace, many of the Welsh leaders complained about the levy being raised to pay Hengest and Horsa for their services. It was felt that there was no longer a need to pay for protection and they refused to make any further contributions. Just as in the heat of summer it is hard to recall the biting cold of winter, so in the calm of peace it is hard to recall the turmoil and suffering of war. An assembly of representatives from the Welsh kingdoms withdrew their support for Vortigern and his policy and, as a result, he informed Hengest's men that the agreement was ended and the payments would stop.

When Hengest heard that the Welsh were refusing to supply his warriors with the food and other provisions they were due, he went to Britain to assess the situation and to talk with Vortigern who was facing increasing internal opposition. Hengest offered to fight for the King against his opponents and a deal was struck by which Hengest would receive land in Kent in payment for his support. Word was sent back across the sea to Angeln ordering them to send more men. When reinforcements arrived Hengest and his twin Horsa led the rebellion and drove away those who sought to overthrow the King. Then Vortigern, concerned at his increasing reliance on Hengest and fearing that he was losing the support of his countrymen, turned on Hengest who again sent for more men and told them of the worthlessness of the Welsh and of the excellence of the land. A large force of picked men was assembled and sent across the sea in nineteen ships to help the others. The warriors came from three powerful nations of Germany; the Engle, the Saxons and the Jutes. From the Jutes came the people of Kent and the people of the Isle of Wight and the mainland opposite Wight. From the Saxons came the East Saxons and the South Saxons and the West Saxons. From Angeln came the East Engle, Middle Engle, Mercians and all the Northumbrians. Such was to be the extent of the migration from Angeln to Britain over the succeeding years, that when it was finished, the country of Angeln stood empty.

The First
England
(the land of the Engle)
at the end of 4th century

Jutes

Jællinge

North Sea

Engle

Rendsburg

Eider

Myrgings

Weser

Elbe

Ems

Saxons

England

Late 5th century

The West Engle were called Mercians
which means 'borderers' or
'dwellers on the march'.

North Engle

Mercians

Lindesey

Middle
Engle

East
Engle

East
Saxons

Jutes

West
Saxons

South Saxons

Jutes

ENGLAND
9th Century

Strathclyde

Welsh

Bernicia

Northumberland

Deira

Gwynedd

Powys

Dyfed

Welsh

Mercia

Northfolk

East Anglia

Southfolk

Essex

Middlesex

Kent

Wessex

Sussex

Welsh

Hengest and Horsa were the sons of Wihtgils, the son of Witta, the son of Wecta, the son of Woden. From Woden sprang many of the southern kings and all the Northumbrian royal family. Hengest and Horsa fought Vortigern in the place called Aegelsthrep (Aylesford, Kent). Hengest was victorious but Horsa was killed and Oisc succeeded to the kingdom and ruled with Hengest. Two years later Hengest and Oisc fought the Welsh at a place called Crecganforf (Crayford, Kent) and killed four thousand of the enemy. The Welsh abandoned Kent and fled to London in great terror.

Hengest fought in many battles in the south and in the north of Britain and he put the Welsh to flight through fire and the sword's edge. Hengest and Oisc fought them near Wippedesfleot and killed twelve Welsh lords. One of their own thanes named Wipped was also slain there. Eight years later the Anglo-Saxons again fought the Welsh and captured innumerable spoils, and the Welsh fled as one flees from fire, and the Anglo-Saxons became rulers of their own lands in Britain and the dominant political and military force. Behind the warriors came the settlers who farmed the new land as they had the old.

Not all territory was won by force of arms. As the Anglo-Saxon population increased it began to displace the Welsh who gradually migrated to areas where they were dominant. As the Anglo-Saxons advanced and created new farmsteads the Welsh names for settlements and local features of the landscape were either Anglicised or given English names. Woods, streams and settlements became known to the English by names derived from the names of the tribe, family or individual who owned the land, or lived on it, or to the use to which it was put, or its physical description. Some woods, hills and springs were given names that linked them with the Gods. (For example, Tuesley [Tiw] and Thursley [Thunor] in Surrey, Wednesfield and Wednesbury [Woden] in Staffordshire. Harrow-on-the-Hill in its earliest form means 'the holy place of the Gumeningas'; the Gumeningas being a tribe.)

The names of Romano-British towns and the Welsh names for some features such as large rivers were retained as these had been learned from the Welsh by the early English settlers. While it is easy to change a local name it is more difficult to change the name of something that is known to many people over a wide area. A similar process occurred when the English settled in North America. Indian names were retained for mountains and large rivers but smaller geographical features and settlements were, generally, given English names. More North American Indian words entered the English language as the result of the conquest of North America than Welsh words entered the English language as a result of the conquest and settlement of much of Britain.

With the exception of large towns, the place names of a country rarely change while the long-standing population remains on the land and there is little mixing with the new settlers. For example Wales, Scotland and, at one time, Ireland were absorbed into the English state and the population of those countries now speak English but the place names are, with few exceptions, not English. The main exception is Scotland where the Anglo-Saxons settled much of the lowland, particularly in the east.

Another indication of displacement or mixing of populations is the extent to which words from the 'old' language enter the 'new' language. Other than place names very few Welsh/Celtic words have entered the English language.

The fundamental nature of society in the part of Britain that was to become England was completely changed during the period of Anglo-Saxon migration and settlement. It was not just a military conquest by a small elite but a massive migration. There is some debate concerning the extent to which the Anglo-Saxon population replaced the Welsh, or Romano-British, population. Celtic nationalists tend to be drawn to two opposing views on this matter, the first arguing that the Anglo-Saxons drove the Welsh from their land, while the second suggests that the Welsh-Celtic population remained in place and absorbed the comparatively few Anglo-Saxon invaders. The mechanisms by which a small Anglo-Saxon warrior elite was able to bring about such profound and rapid change in every aspect of society, and at all levels, is never adequately explained. Many of those propagating the absorption theory are engaged in a form of cultural warfare in which they are attempting to reverse the effects of a historical process by trying to persuade the English that they are really Celts. Such propaganda has had some success amongst the young, and particularly with those who might be called 'New Agers', who like to think of the British Celts as nice peace-loving people rather than as war-like people who were not very successful at fighting wars. (The British-Celts are also often, and incorrectly, credited with having constructed the ancient earthworks and stone circles of Britain.)

There are also those who, for ideological reasons, favour the liberal, ethnic integration and cultural enrichment interpretation of British history. This politically correct view, from which academics are not exempt, argues that English society has always been ethnically and culturally mixed and that contemporary immigration into Britain of people from all over the world is merely a continuation of that process of cultural enrichment and not one to be resisted or challenged. Such advocates tend to be uninterested in what actually happened and take as obvious and irrefutable their assertion that multi-cultural, multi-ethnic societies are a good thing. Their melting-pot theory is similar to the one that has often applied to North American society, where most of the early immigrants were either English or Europeans who could easily be absorbed into an Anglo-Saxon society. Later the numbers and cultural differences became so great that the process of assimilation broke down. But that is another story.

Support for the view that there was a large-scale Anglo-Saxon migration comes from research based on the distribution of ABO blood groups. Group *A* is more common among Germanic North Europeans, and group *O* more frequent among 'Celtic British'. Blood group *O* is more common in Ireland and the west of Great Britain, while *A* is more frequent in East Anglia and the East and South East. A genetic map produced by Kopec (1970) from the records of half a million blood donors, showed a high incidence of *A*, and a low incidence of *O*, in East Anglia. It also showed the incidence of *A* decreasing and that of *O* increasing from east to west and from south to north.

Another study (Roberts et al., 1981) showed that if the gradient is looked at closely it is seen to contain within it a patchwork of gene pools which sometimes are, or were, separated by geographical barriers such as mountains, rivers marshes or forests. Where geographical factors were not the cause of the enclaves it must be presumed that they were due to cultural barriers. For example in Cumbria, where there is a high incidence of group O, it is possible to identify areas high in group A whose place names are of Norwegian origin.

That such a gradient and patchwork still exist would seem to indicate that one wave of migrants displaced an earlier group which then tended to move west or north west and that the mixing of the population was not so great as to produce an even distribution of blood groups.

For the most part the Welsh and English appear to have lived apart and retained their own languages and customs. The English and the Welsh were proud of their history, achievements and way of life. They did not praise any gods but their own or tell of the brave deeds of any lords but their own or see the worth of any society but their own. They were confident and noble peoples who, while they had an independent existence, had no wish or need to adopt the customs of others. As a result there was comparatively little contact between the two peoples who, for the most part, regarded the other with hostility. There was some trade between them and later, when the English kingdoms had become well established, there were occasions when English and Welsh leaders formed alliances for the purpose of confronting a common Welsh or English enemy. However, during the period of Anglo-Saxon expansion, most English trade was with their fellow countrymen in England, and with the Germanic peoples across the North Sea. Likewise the Welsh traded mainly with their fellow countrymen in Britain, and with Ireland and Brittany. Both sides also retained their trade links with the Roman Empire.

Summary

The evidence for ethnic, linguistic, social and cultural changes in much of Britain during the fifth and sixth centuries is overwhelming. The Anglo-Saxon settlement which brought this about, and led to the creation of England took many generations to complete and took different forms in different places at different times. It occurred in several stages.

a. The first stage was the growth of Anglo-Saxon settlements close to Roman garrison towns during the Roman occupation of Britain. Most of those settlements remained after the withdrawal of Roman forces and acted as focal points for later migration.

b. When the Romans withdrew from Britain in an attempt to recover from their defeat by Germanic tribes in Gaul, they made easier the movement of Germanic tribes to Britain. After the initial heavy Saxon raids there was a gradual peaceful settlement, by various Germanic peoples, of the coastal areas of what is now East Anglia.

c. The second half of the fifth century was a period of steady military conquest and migration in which the early Anglo-Saxon settlements formed a secure base area and bridgehead. The Welsh either migrated from, or were driven from, most of eastern, southern, and south-eastern Britain, and at the end of that century the land east of a line from The Wash to the Isle of Wight was in English hands. The Welsh managed to halt the advance for a generation at the Battle (or Siege) of Mount Badon where they enjoyed a rare victory over the Anglo-Saxons and they may have recaptured some territory. Where and when the battle took place is unknown but two of several suggested locations are a hill just east of Bath, and Bradbury, south east of Swindon. Suggested dates for the battle range from 490 to 516.

d. After a generation of stability, in which the Anglo-Saxons were able to consolidate their position, they advanced once again, but more quickly than before. Many of the Welsh fled into the inhospitable lands on the western fringe of Britain or migrated across the sea to Brittany. This last stage of conquest and settlement took several generations to complete and consisted of a succession of campaigns and rapid advances. Large areas of land were won and it is likely that more of the Welsh remained than had done so during earlier campaigns. Most of those who stayed probably continued to work the land but were absorbed into Anglo-Saxon society as the lowest social class. With the exception of Wales and some western regions (such as Cornwall, Dorset and Cumbria), the Welsh only survived as self-governing communities for a short while in small enclaves.

It took the Anglo-Saxons many generations to win all the land that became England. Their conquest was different from, and more thorough than, any since. In most of England, and especially in the lowland areas, the changes they brought were very deep and widespread. Their system of law and administration, and the principles that underpinned it, helped form the foundations of the institutions we have today in England and other Anglo-Saxon societies. The mode of agriculture, holding of land, construction of buildings, methods of burial and grave goods, place names, religion and language, all changed with their arrival.

The Anglo-Saxon conquest and settlement was more thorough, and its effects more far reaching, than any since. It was not merely the migration of a small ruling elite, but a massive tribal migration which, in many places, and especially in the east, displaced the earlier population. The Engle, Saxons and Jutes came to Britain as warriors and as settlers and they came in very large numbers. They were able to populate most of the fertile lowlands of England and contain the Welsh who occupied the frontier lands in the west and north-west. The land formerly occupied by the Engle was left deserted when the period of migration ended. The king, his family, companions, and all his people went to Britain. Some went to the lands to the south of the River Humber (Southumbrians) while some went to the lands north of the Humber (Northumbrians). They eventually occupied the east coast of Britain as far north as the Firth of Forth, and many of the Lowland Scots are descended from the Engle and their language, Scots, is a dialect of English.

The Engle were almost certainly the most numerous of all the Germanic people who crossed the sea to Britain and, mainly for that reason, when the settlers merged into one nation, sharing a single country, the English gave their name to the people, the country and the language.

Later invasions by Scandinavians and Normans had a significant impact on English society, and, in the case of the Normans, on the language and political institutions, but they did not fundamentally change the population or the popular culture of the country. The Danish armies were comparatively small but they won political control of much of England. Many Danes migrated to England and created new communities but there was not a mass migration of the whole Danish people as there had been with the English, or even a very large part of it. Their number in England was comparatively small and gradually they were absorbed into English society and the English population, with which they had much in common. The Normans, in part a Germanic people and not 'French' as is often thought, were a small military ruling elite who took over the existing institutions of the English state. In many ways they were less advanced than the English, but in at least one battle more militarily successful and that, in the short term, is what counts. It took some time for the English population to absorb the Norman elite and their allies but they eventually did so. Those individuals who today have a family name of Norman origin may care to reflect that their ancestor, to whom the name was first given, was very probably the English servant of a Norman lord and did not, as is often claimed, 'come over with the Normans'.

The reason for the comparatively swift absorption of Scandinavians and Normans into the English nation was that they were comparatively small in number and ethnically and culturally similar to the Anglo-Saxons.

The Anglo-Saxon *Rune Poem*

The Anglo-Saxon *Rune Poem* is the most complete and accomplished account of rune names and their meanings. It consists of twenty-nine stanzas, each of which contains words of worldly wisdom (gnomic statements) and conveys the meaning of a rune in a way designed to aid the memory. The original manuscript (Cotton Otho B10) containing the text of the poem was destroyed by fire in 1731, along with many others. Fortunately it had been copied and printed by George Hicks in his *Thesaurus*, and thus the most detailed of the extant rune poems managed to survive.

Many of those who write about runes, and are interested in the meaning they had for heathens, tend to either ignore the Anglo-Saxon *Rune Poem* or treat the English futhorc as being of less interest than those of the Elder or the Younger Futhark. Some people find the linking of runes with the Vikings and their warlike ways attractive and inspiring. However, many others, particularly women, are put off by the association. This is a great pity as English heathenism, of which runes are an important part, placed far more emphasis on the importance of the Earth Goddess (Nerthus or Frig) than did the later Norse variants. English heathenism seems to have offered a far more balanced view of the powers and importance of the Gods and Goddesses and was not distorted by the influence of a society in which the cult of the warrior had become all-pervading. For this reason those who have an aversion to runes because they are, "fed up with having the Vikings pushed down their throats", may find English runes, and English heathenism, more attractive than the Norse variants. This does not mean that the Norse version of Germanic mythology can be ignored, it clearly cannot. The *Poetic* and *Prose Eddas*, as recorded by Snorri Sturluson, are an invaluable source of information without which the whole subject would be shrouded in darkness. We should use Norse mythology as a guide and a source of information when trying to understand English heathen beliefs while bearing in mind that they from a much later period.

While there has obviously been some tinkering with the Anglo-Saxon *Rune Poem* by the monks who recorded it, and references to the Christian god have been inserted, they are easy to spot and can either be ignored or, as elsewhere in this book, removed and replaced with the appropriate heathen god. An example of Christian tinkering is said to be revealed in the name given to the third rune in the futhorc. The Norwegian and Icelandic poems give the name *þurs*, which means 'giant' or 'demon' while the English name is *þorn* (thorn). As giants are associated with evil in Germanic heathen lore, it has been argued that this is a clear example of Christians removing references to things with heathen connotations and replacing them with innocuous substitutes. Such may be the case but it is also possible that the English poem records the 'original' meaning and that it was the Scandinavians who changed it later. If the English did change the name it may have been done by heathens and the new description may have been thought to be a more clever and sophisticated way of alluding to evil. The thorn rune does after all look more like a thorn than a giant and it has been suggested that the shape of some runes is a clue to their name.

The early English seem to have enjoyed riddles (ninety-five of them are recorded in the *Exeter Book*) so perhaps some of the *Rune Poem* stanzas should be looked at as riddles. One of the best known of the Anglo-Saxon riddles is:

> *A creature came where warriors were sitting in council, men wise in mind. It had two ears and one eye, two feet and twelve-hundred heads, a back and a belly and two hands, arms and shoulders, one neck and two sides. Say what I am called.*

The answer is a one-eyed garlic seller. Many of the riddles are more profound than this example but it does demonstrate a sense of humour. There is often much more to Anglo-Saxon verse than is at first apparent, so perhaps some of the stanzas of the rune poems should be looked at in that light. The study of runes need not be as serious and gloomy as some people think it ought to be.

It should be borne in mind that if the Anglo-Saxon *Rune Poem* and the information it contains is to be dismissed as unreliable because it was recorded by Christians, then most of the other information we have about runes, and much else besides, including the Norse myths, should also be dismissed. What would be left?

The Origin of Runes

The original purpose of runes is not known but one theory suggests that over a long period a number of symbols were devised to represent mankind's perception of creation and his place in it. There were symbols for the mysterious forces of nature and for the gods who controlled or influenced them. The signs represented ideas and beliefs that were a distillation of the accumulated wisdom of the ages. For the rune masters the runes remained essentially a means for representing mysteries but for the uninitiated it was the runic signs that were mysterious, and because of that the signs themselves also came to be called runes.

Some runic symbols are very ancient and may date from the time of a proto-Indo-European language when they were used as an early form of writing, the symbols being used as ideograms. The system of writing evolved and developed until either spontaneously, or as the result of contact with another culture, a revised and formalised system was created and adopted. That first formal system may have been the Elder Futhark but there may have been an earlier one from which it evolved. It is not known where or precisely when the Elder Futhark came into being but archaeological evidence suggests that it was probably in, or just south of, the Jutland peninsula during the first half of the first millennium C.E. It seems to have been during this period that the rune signs were given a specific order, acquired a specific sound value and were divided into three groups of eight. Such divisions are called 'ættir', and they were probably made for magical reasons, and seem to have been of some importance.

It is reasonable to suppose that the Elder Futhark was created primarily for linguistic purposes and that most of the runes included in it had a name that started with a sound needed for the futhark. The requirements of the futhark were the same as for the alphabet; a word was needed to represent, or illustrate, each of the basic or simple sounds used in the language in much the same way we use apple for 'a', ball for 'b', cat for 'c', etc. When it was not possible to use a rune name starting with the correct sound they used instead a rune name that contained the required sound. For example the rune Ing represents the sound 'ng', and eolhxsecg (elksedge) has the same phonetic value as the Roman letter 'x'.

It seems unlikely that there were twenty-four runes already in existence with names suitable for inclusion in such a system and the names of some runes may have been changed and new runic signs devised for the purpose. Some symbols were probably borrowed from the Etruscan alphabet and named according to the needs of the time.

Whatever the original purpose of runes it would seem evident that they came to represent and express a moral code or guide to life. The values they promote were by no means unique to English society and seem to have been common to other heathen societies of that time. When a society has to be continually prepared for war it is natural that it should extol values and attitudes that promote a fighting spirit, as is done in the runic system. Most runes are, however, concerned with other areas of human activity and the needs of individuals in times of stress and hardship. All the runic virtues can serve as a guide to all members of society. Loyalty, courage, honesty, stoicism and generosity are virtues that everyone can strive for, just as all should value friendships and seek knowledge and wisdom.

A moral code is something that seems to be lacking in modern heathenism where the only moral imperative that can be widely agreed upon is, "Do what you will but harm none". Many heathens look with favour on the first part of the stricture but some find it difficult to observe the second part. That heathen morality should be expressed in such a limited and inadequate way probably demonstrates the impossibility of agreeing on anything more substantial. Perhaps the runic values could serve as a basis for a heathen moral code, if only it were possible to agree what those values are.

The Meaning of 'Rune'

The word 'rūn' in Old English was used in several ways and can be taken to have meant (a) 'a letter', 'writing', (b) 'a private thought', 'an idea', (c) 'a whisper', 'a sound'. According to J. M. Kemble (*On Anglo-Saxon Runes*) the original meaning of 'rune' as a noun was probably 'mystery' or 'secret', and as a verb 'to whisper', or 'to tell secrets'. This tends to support the view that the idea represented by the rune symbol was of first importance and that the symbol and its name were of secondary importance. A further reason for believing in the primacy of the runic idea is that runemasters used many different shapes and names to represent runes but the ideas remained fairly constant and continued to reflect the values and perceptions of Germanic heathen society.

Rune Symbols

Most runic symbols consist of straight vertical and diagonal lines, and were originally designed to be cut or scratched onto hard surfaces. The vertical line of a rune is called a stem. In Scandinavia the vertical line is called a 'staver' and the diagonal line a 'bistaver'. This can cause confusion as the pieces of wood on which runes are sometimes cut are, in English, called 'staves'.

The symbols incorporated into the earliest known runic alphabet (Elder Futhark) were particularly suited to being scratched or carved onto wood as they have no horizontal lines which might either be lost in the wood grain or cause the wood to split. In other words the vertical and diagonal lines of the runes remained distinct from the horizontal lines of the grain and easy to read. 'Letter Runes' are thus easier to mark on wood, and easier to read, than most other symbols. Runes were also engraved on swords, cut into stone monuments, marked on funeral urns, and stamped on coins. Later they were recorded in manuscripts and it is from that source we have learnt, if only imperfectly, their meanings and phonetic values.

Letter Runes: The Futhark and Futhorc

The early form of the runic script contains twenty-four runes and is known as the Elder Futhark. The name 'futhark' is derived from the first six runes of the sequence. ('th' is represented by the thorn rune.) The runes of the Elder Futhark, are often found divided into three groups of eight but the original significance of such divisions is not known, although many people have guessed at it and elaborate theories have been put forward to explain it. The groups, or families of runes, are called 'ætt' (singular) and 'ættir' (plural) and were often marked by vertical lines of dots (usually two dots) between the eighth and ninth, and sixteenth and seventeenth runes. The later Norse Futharks of sixteen runes, which are a reduced and modified version of the Elder Futhark, are sometimes found divided into two groups of eight.

There is an English and a Frisian Futhorc which are expanded versions of the Elder Futhark and reflect some of the common developments in the English and Frisian languages. The later addition of several mainly Northumbrian runes brought the total number of available English runes to thirty-three, but for the purposes of this book the Anglo-Saxon Futhorc will contain the twenty-nine runes given in the *Rune Poem*. It should be noted that the English system is called the Anglo-Saxon Futhorc, not Futhark.

Most English futhorcs are not divided into ættir but those that are follow the divisions of the Elder Futhark. Anglo-Saxon runes usually run from left to right but they can run from right to left, and some inscriptions mix the two with, for example, one line reading one way and the next line running the other way. Runes can also be reversed or inverted and are sometimes found joined or combined with other runes and are then called bind-runes. Such runes are fairly common in Scandinavia but are only rarely found in England. Bind-runes might be a form of abbreviation used by the carver to save time or space, or they may be due to the need of the runemaster, perhaps for magical purposes, to have a certain number of runes in an inscription or a word, or a line.

Although runemasters tended to follow the traditional shapes and conventions, there are variations and some of these may have been due to the nature of the material on which the inscription was made or to the space available. For example some of the runes found engraved on stone monuments, or written on parchment, do not consist entirely of straight lines. The reason probably being that it was quicker and easier to cut corners and there was no functional reason to keep the lines straight.

From the time of the earliest known inscription there have been variations in the number of Letter Runes, in their shape and the order in which they appear. It seems reasonable to conclude that individual runes and the system as a whole have been subject to an evolutionary process since the time of their first use and that runes do not have a definitive shape, order, sound, or number and that no one system is better, more authentic, or possessed of greater magical powers than any other.

One result of the modern tendency to try to impose order on what may have been a disorderly system is that many craftsmen have been labelled as stupid or careless when their ancient inscriptions have not obeyed modern rules. For example the Thames Scramasax Futhorc has some unusual variations which are sometimes explained away as mistakes.

Although it seems probable that the root meaning of rune is 'a mystery', or 'an idea', the history of the development of runes is closely linked to the requirements of language and the periods during which runes underwent the greatest change tended to coincide with important stages in the evolution of the various Germanic languages. The expansion of the Elder Futhark of twenty-four runes to the Anglo-Saxon Futhorc of up to thirty-three runes, and the later reduction of the Norse futharks to sixteen runes, were quite drastic changes which involved the creation of many variants, the substitution of others, and the introduction of new rune shapes. Such changes indicate that during the later stages of their development runes were important as a form of writing but the evidence for this does not mean that Letter Runes ceased to be used for magical purposes. On the contrary it may have been seen as increasing their mystery. It is also probable that the runes not included in the futhark continued to be used for magical purposes.

Table of Anglo-Saxon Runes

Runes and Roman characters are not easily substituted one for another because some of the sounds used in spoken Old English cannot be represented by a single Roman letter. However it is possible to find approximate values and, in the table opposite, they have been given under each rune. Where there are two vowels together (diphthongs) they should be pronounced as two vowels but slurred together.

The Old English and Modern English rune names are given beneath the Roman characters. The Old English rune names are those given in the *Rune Poem*.

A number of English 'pseudo' runes have not been included in the table as they were late additions which were probably introduced solely for the purpose of meeting the needs of a changing language and to provide runes for the Roman letters Q, V, K and Z, which are not represented in the futhorc. If the pseudo runes had esoteric values we can only guess what they might have been.

Instead of inventing new runes to fill the gaps it is possible to use some of the existing runes to do the job. In Old English the letters CW were used to represent Q. Tolkien advocated doing the same with runes and used ᚩ , CW, to represent Q. K can be represented by ᚳ , C; V by ᚢ , U; and the one letter left unaccounted for, Z, can be represented by the yew rune, ᛇ , for no other reason than similarity of appearance.

Anglo-Saxon Futhorc

ᚠᚢᚦᚨᚱᛣᚷᚹᚻᚾᛁᛄᛇᛈᛉᛋᛏᛒᛖᛗᛚᛝᛞᚪᚫᚣᛡᛠ

ᚠ	ᚢ	ᚦ	ᚠ	ᚱ
f	u	th	o	r
feoh	ur	þorn	os	rad
wealth	aurochs	thorn	mouth	riding
ᚳ	ᚷ	ᚹ	ᚻ	ᚾ
c	g	w	h	n
cen	gyfu	wynn	hægl	nyd
torch	gift	joy	hail	need
ᛁ	ᛄ	ᛇ	ᛈ	ᛉ
i	j	eo	p	x
is	ger	eoh	peorð	eolhxsecg
ice	harvest	ycw	hearth	elksedge
ᛋ	ᛏ	ᛒ	ᛖ	ᛗ
s	t	b	e	m
sigel	Tir	beorc	eh	man
sun	Tiw	birch	horse	man
ᛚ	ᛝ	ᛟ	ᛞ	ᚪ
l	ng	œ	d	a
lagu	Ing	eþel	dæg	ac
water	Ing	homeland	day	oak
ᚫ	ᚣ	ᛡ	ᛠ	
œ	y	ia	ea	
œsc	yr	ior	ear	
ash	weapon	beaver	grave	

Good must struggle with evil; youth must
struggle with old age; life must struggle with
death; light must struggle with darkness,
army with army, foe with foe,
enemy with enemy struggle
over land and each put the
blame upon the other.

The wise man must always give
thought to the conflicts of this world;
the criminal must hang to pay the price
for the crime he has committed against
mankind. Allfather alone knows
where the souls of the dead go. The
shape of the future after death is
dark and unknowable, for no-one
returns to tell us for certain what
it is like. The Bright Citadel that
is Heaven, where the Gods live
with their victorious people,
is a mystery.

The Anglo-Saxon Rune Poem

feoh

feoh bȳþ frofur   fira gehƿylcum
sceal ðeah manna gehƿylc   miclun hȳt dǣlan
gif he ƿile for ðrihtne   domes hleotan.

Wealth is a comfort to all men.
Yet each must give freely to
win glory in heaven.

Be open-handed and use wealth to
benefit the living. Treasure in a barrow
makes a fine lair for a dragon but it is giving,
not hoarding, that gains respect on Earth
and glory in Heaven.

Wealth brings wolves from the woods.

ur

uṛ bẏþ anmod   an oꝼeꝛhẏꝛneð
ꝼelaꝼꝛecne deoꝛ   ꝼeohteþ mi hoꝛnum
mæꝛe moꝛꝛtapa   þæt iꝼ modiᵹ puht.

The Aurochs is determined and armed above.
Fierce and bold it fights with horns.
Monster moor-stepper, it is a mighty creature.

Strength is a great asset, made greater
still if he who has it is seen to be
fearless and well armed.

Strength is a great asset, but it must be
tempered with courage and determination.
One brave man can kill an aurochs.

Strength is a great asset, but it must be
tempered with wisdom and cunning.
One clever man can kill an aurochs.

þorn

þorn byþ ðearle rcearp   ðegna gehƿylcum
anrengg ýr ýrýl   ungemetun reþe
manna gehƿylcun   ðe him mid rerteð.

Thorn is very sharp for all men.
Struggling with them is painful for any warrior.
They are severe to those who live among them.

Fiends are cruel to those who keep their company.

Evil does harm to those who practice it.

os

os býþ onðfruma   ælcpe fppæce
pirðomef pnaþu   an pitena fnofun
anð eopla gehpam   eaðnýf anð tohiht.

A god is the origin of all speech.
Wisdom's prop and wise men's comfort,
and for every man a blessing and a joy.

Woden is God of Wisdom, God of War and
God of the Dead. He is a shaman and a healer,
and has the power of prophecy. He gave an eye
to drink from the Spring of Knowledge and
Understanding. He is wise beyond the
understanding of mankind and from him,
the one-eyed god, came the runes and the
power of speech. On dark and stormy
nights he rides across the sky with the
Valkyries, the Daughters of Night,
in a hunt for lost souls.

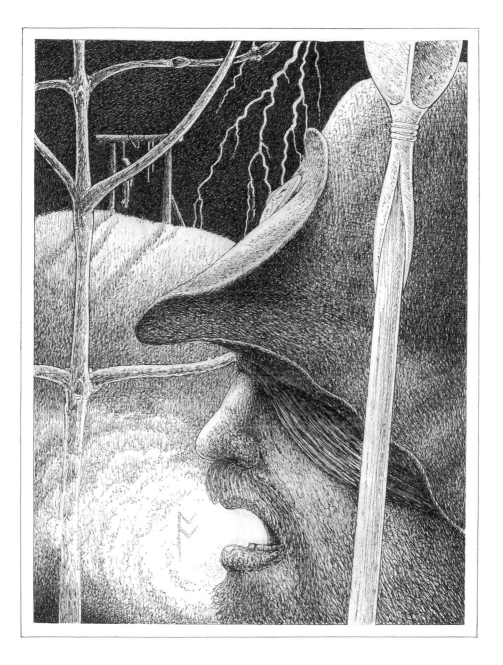

rad

það býþ on pecýðe   þinca gehþýlcum
ƒeƒte anð ƒþiþhþæt   ðam ðe ƒitteþ onuƒan
meaþe mægenheaþðum   oƒeþ milþaþaƒ.

Riding in the hall is very pleasant but
for the warrior sitting on a strong horse
covering the mile-paths it is very hard.

Before you take to the road give thought
to the hardships, as well as the rewards,
that await you. Anticipation should
be the first step on a long journey.

It is easier to dream than to perform
the task, but those who undertake the
journey determine the affairs of mankind.
Thought should precede action, not replace it.

Those who travel widely need their wits
about them. Fools should stay at home.

cen

cen bẏþ cƿicena ᵹehƿam   cuþ on ᵹẏne
blac anᵹ beoꞃhtlic   bẏꞃneþ oꝼtuꞃt
ᵹæꞃ hi æþelinᵹaꞃ   inne ꞃeꞃtaþ.

Torch to all living creatures is clear by its fire.
Shiny and bright it burns most often
where leaders choose to rest.

Torch is a beacon around which those of
common purpose can gather together.
Wisdom and hope are the flames of the
torch of leadership. Courage makes
it burn more brightly.

gyfu

gȳfu ȝumena bȳþ   ȝlenȝ anð heᵽenȳᵱ
ᵽᵱaþu an ᵽȳnþᵱcȳᵱe   an ᵽᵱæcna ȝehᵱam
an anð ætᵱiᵱᵼ   ðe bȳþ oᵱna leaᵱ.

Giving is for men glory and acclaim,
support and honour, and for the needy
a help and sustenance that is otherwise lacking.

Be open-handed with those you invite under
your roof and you will earn their respect,
and that of your fellows. When others
share what they have with you, however
little it may be, show them respect.
It is often easier to give than to receive.

No person is so rich that he will not
welcome thanks for a gift given.

wynn

ƿenne bruceþ   ðe can ƿeana lyt
sareſ and ſorge   and him ſylfa hæfþ
blæd an blyſſe   and eac byrga geniht.

Joyful is he who has little want,
soreness and sorrow, and has for himself
plenty and bliss and a comfortable dwelling.

Joyful are those who recognise good fortune when
it is with them. To know joy, you must also know
sorrow, but do not seek it out as Wyrd has enough
for us all. The sorrow of others is not hard
to find for those who have eyes to see.

hagl

hægl byþ hpituſt coɲɲa hpýɲſt hiꞇ oſ heoſoɲeſ lýſꞇe
pealcaþ hiꞇ piɲdeſ ſcuɲa peoɲþeþ hiꞇ ꞇo pæꞇeɲe ſýꝛꝛan.

Hail is the whitest of grains. It descends from heaven's air
and swirls in the wind. Soon it returns to water.

Hail, the white fiend, the coldest
of grains, drops suddenly from
heaven and sweeps across
the land, laying waste the
fine crops standing
ripe in the
field.

nyd

nȳð bẏþ neaꞃu on bꞃeoꞅꞇan þeoꞃþeþ hi ðeah oꞃꞇ niþa beaꞃꞃnum
ꞇo helpe anð ꞇo hæle ꞡehƿæþꞃe ꞡiꞃ hi hiꞅ hlẏꞅꞇaþ æꞃoꞃ.

Need pains the heart yet it is often a help and salvation
to the sons of men if they attend to it soon.

Hardship, like guilt, causes us discomfort but it
can also bring contentment if we confront it.

Need of friendship can be more painful
than the need of food and warmth.

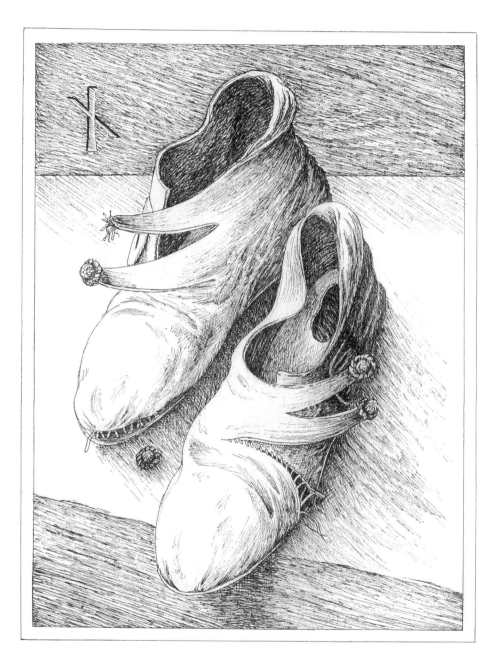

I

is

ıſ bẏþ ofenceald   ungemetum ſlidon
glıſnaþ glæſ hluttur   gimmum gelicuſt
flon fonſte gewonuht   fægen anſyne.

Ice is very cold and terribly slippery.
It glistens like glass, gleams like gems,
a floor wrought with frost, fair to the sight.

Much of what we desire is
difficult or dangerous to gain,
painful to hold, and easily
slips from our grasp.
What looks resplendent
from afar is often
dull to the
touch.

ger

ᵹeᵹ bÿþ ᵹumena hiht   ðon ᵹoð læteþ
haliᵹ heoᵹoneᵹ cÿninᵹ   hᵹuᵹan ᵹÿllan
beoᵹhte bleða   beoᵹnum anð ðeaᵹᵹum.

Fruitful year, is the hope of men, when Frig,
heaven's queen, makes the earth
give forth bright crops for rich and poor.

Frig is Earth and of Earth. She is her own daughter
and is known by many names. Frig is the Goddess of
fertility and love; she brings us the fruits of the earth
and the fruits of our loins. She is Goddess of the
harvest and Mother of Mankind. She is generous
with her gifts; use them wisely and care for
her, so that she is able to care for
those who come after us.

eoh

eoh bẏþ uᴛan   unᵲmeþe ᴛᵲeop
heaᵲᴅ hᵲuᵲan fæᵲᴛ   hẏᵲᴅe fẏᵲeᵲ
pẏᵲᴛᵲumun unᴅeᵲᵲᵲeþẏᴅ   ᵲẏnan on eþle.

The Yew is outwardly an unsmooth tree,
hard and fast in the earth, the keeper of fire,
roots twisted in the earth, a pleasure on the land.

The yew is very strong and long of life.
Its roots and branches, like the Web of Wyrd,
reach out into the seven worlds.
The yew is always green.

HEAVEN

LIGHT ELVES   DWARFS

THE MIDDLE ENCLOSURE

GIANTS   DARK ELVES

HELL

peorð

peorð byþ symble   plega and hlehter
plancum   ðar wigan sittaþ
on beorsele   bliþe ætsomne.

Peorth is ever entertainment and laughter
for the proud, where warriors sit
cheerfully together in the beer-hall.

Ease and openness are joys to be had when
kin or companions sit together playing,
riddling and storytelling around the
hearth in relaxed friendship.

eolhx

eolhxꞅecᵹ eaꞃð hæꝥꝥ   oꞅꞇuꞃꞇ on ꝼenne
ᵹexeð on ᵹaꞇuꞃe   ᵹunðaꝥ ᵹꞃimme
bloðe bꞃeneð   beoꞃna ᵹehꝥýlcne
ðe him æniᵹne   onꝼenᵹ ᵹeðeð

Elksedge most often lives in the fen,
growing in water; it grimly wounds
and burns with blood every person
who grasps it.

Be wary even in times of need.
Grabbing quickly for support at
that which comes to hand
can bring pain and sorrow.

sigel

ᚱᛖᚷᛖᛚ ᚱᛖᛗᚪᚾᚾᚢᛗ   ᛋᚣᛗᛒᛚᛖ ᛒᛁᚦ ᚩᚾ ᚻᛁᚻᛏᛖ
ᚦᚩᚾᚾ ᚻᛁ ᚻᛁᚾᛖ ᚠᛖᚱᛁᚪᚦ   ᚩᚠᛖᚱ ᚠᛁᛋᚳᛖᛋ ᛒᛖᚦ
ᚩᚦ ᚻᛁ ᛒᚱᛁᛗᚻᛖᚾᚷᛖᛋᛏ   ᛒᚱᛁᚾᚷᛖᚦ ᛏᚩ ᛚᚪᚾᛞᛖ.

Sun ever proves a joy to seamen
when they cross the fish-bath-sea,
till the brine-steed brings them to land.

Sun brings a fair journey and good fortune.
Her bright light chases away fear, and
warms the sea and soil.

Tir

Tiꞃ biþ ꞇacna ꞅum   healeðþ ꞇꞃȳꝛa ꝥel
ꝥiþ æþelinᵹaꞅ   a biþ on ꝼæꞃȳlðe
oꝼeꞃ nihꞇa ᵹeniꝝu   næꝼꝛe ꞅꝛiceþ

Tiw is a guiding mark. He keeps trust
with all men, is ever on His path above
the night's mists and never fails.

Tiw is the warrior's friend; God of courage,
aggression and glory. Like the guiding star
that bears his name, he shines out of the darkness
and is always there for those who need him.

Tiw, the Sky Father, and bringer of glory, was the
first of the gods of the shining stronghold that is
Heaven. Other gods have powers that were once
his, but he still watches over us as provider;
the God of order and justice. Tiw is unflinching
in battle and in all he does. Warriors and
travellers look to his brightly burning light.

beorc

beoɲc bÿþ bleða leaſ   beɲeþ eſne ſɲa ðeah
ɯanaſ buɯan ɯuððeɲ   biþ on ɯelȝum pliɯiȝ
þeah on helme   hɲÿɯeð ſœȝeɲe
ȝeloðen leaſum   lÿſɯe ȝeɯenȝe.

Birch has no fruit: it produces
shoots not seeds. It is glorious in its branches,
its crown well adorned,
heavy with leaves, aloft in the sky.

The Birch is a tree of fertility, healing and magic.
Its branches seem bare of flower and seed, yet it
is very fertile and sprouts many shoots. Woden
marked runes on nine birch twigs then struck an
adder with them, so that it flew into nine parts.

Birch is the wood of rune wands and magic.
Birch is the witches' tree.

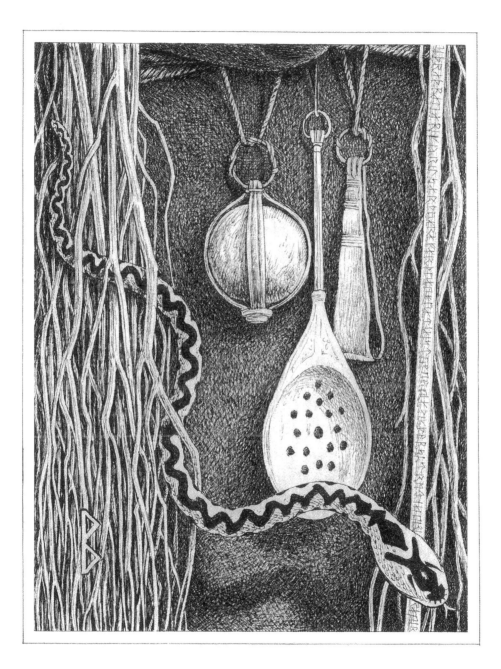

ᛗ

eh

eh byþ for eorlum   æþelinga wyn
hors hofum wlanc   ðær him hæleþe ymb
welege on wicgum   wrixlaþ spræce
an biþ unstyllum   æfre frofur.

Horse, in front of warriors, is the joy of princes.
Steed proud of hoofs, when rich men
on horseback mix words.
To the restless it is ever a comfort.

It is a pleasure to own things that gives pride
in their possession and joy in their use. A horse
provides the opportunity to meet friends,
seek adventure, and visit far-off places.

man

man byþ on myngþe   hir magan leof
rceal þeah anna gehpylc   oðrum rpican
fon ðam dnyhten pyle   dome rine
þæt eanme flærc   eonþan betæcan.

Man in his merriment is dear to his
friends. Yet each is bound to betray his
fellow because Sculd by her decree
commits the wretched flesh to the earth.

Friendship brings great joy and comfort. Value
it highly and tend it carefully, for even those
bonds of friendship that are strong and dear
to you will surely perish. The most solemn
oaths of loyalty are brought to nought by death.
Wyrd has a grave for us all yet we are kept in
doubt until our final day about the end that
awaits us. Sickness, old age or the sword's
edge may end our doomed and transient life.

lagu

lagu byþ leoðum   langrum geþuht
gif hi sculun neþun   on nacan tealtum
an hi sæyþa   sþyþe bregaþ
anð se brim hengest   bridles ne gymeð.

Water to men seems everlasting when they
must venture on an unsteady ship, and the
waves scare them very much, and the
brine-stallion heeds not the bridle.

On earth there is no person who is so confident, so generous with gifts,
so bold in youth, so brave in deeds, or with so loyal a lord, that he can ever
venture over the whale's domain without fear of what Wyrd will bring.
Yet despite the hardships, seafarers return to the salt waves
and undertake journeys to the land of strangers.

Ing

Ingꝥ pæſ æꝼeſꞇ   mꞇð eaſꞇ ðenum
ᵹeſepen ſecᵹun   oꝥ he ſꞇððan eſꞇ
oꝼeſ pæᵹ ᵹepaꞇ   pæn æſꞇeſ pan
ðuſ heaꞃðꞇnᵹaſ   ðone hæle nemðun

Ing was first among the East Danes
seen by men. Then he went back
over the waves his waggon behind him.
Thus the warriors named the hero.

When the English lived in Angel they gave praise to
Mother Earth and called her Nerthus. Ing is the
son of Nerthus, and he and his sister, Eostre, are
called Lord and Lady. Each winter Ing leaves
us and travels over the sea but bonfires,
merriment and burning holly
rouse him from his winter sleep and he
returns with a sheaf of corn as his pillow.
He alone shall unbind the frost's fetters and
drive away winter, so that spring shall return to
give the fields lush grass and the trees a crown of
green. Ing is the God of fertility, peace, and plenty.

epel

epel byþ oferleof   æghþylcum men
gif he mot ðær rihtes   and genyrena on
brucan on bolde   bleaðum oftast

Native land is dear to all men
if they can enjoy its rights and
due respect at home in prosperity.

Native land is freedom and security,
a foundation for contentment and prosperity.

Our homeland was won for us by our forefathers; their blood
is in its soil. All nations need a land of their own in which they
can live by their own laws, and practise their customs in peace and
freedom. Such a land is an inheritance to be treasured and defended.

What has been won at great cost by the brave can be lost cheaply by fools,
and once gone can rarely be regained, and only then at great cost.

dæg

ᛞᚫᚷ ᛒᚣᚦ ᛞᚱᛁᚻᛏᚾᛖᛋ ᚠᚩᚾᛞ   ᛖᚩᚱᛖ ᛗᚪᚾᚾᚢᛗ
ᛗᚫᚱᛖ ᛗᛖᛏᚩᛞᛖᛋ ᛚᛖᚩᚻᛏ   ᛗᚣᚱᚷᚦ ᚪᚾᛞ ᛏᚩᚻᛁᚻᛏ
ᛖᚪᛞᚷᚢᛗ ᚪᚾᛞ ᛖᚪᚱᛗᚢᛗ   ᛖᚪᛚᛚᚢᛗ ᛒᚱᛁᚳᛖ.

Day, dear to mankind, is Heaven's messenger,
Metod's glorious light. It is a comfort
and a joy to rich and poor, useful to all.

The summer solstice marks the longest day,
a time for bonfires and merry-making.

Day is reason and understanding; it brightens
the life of all people and brings many rewards.

ᚪ

ac

ac byþ on eopþan   elða beapnum
  flæsces foðon   fepeþ gelome
 ofep ganotes bæþ   gapsecg fandaþ
hpæþep ac hæbbe   æþele tpeope.

The Oak on earth to the sons of men is
food for flesh. It often fares
over the gannet's bath, and there the ocean tests
whether the oak honours the trust we place in it.

We enjoy the benefit of acorns that fell to earth
before our birth. We eat the flesh of pigs that
feed on the fruit, and we build ships from the timber.

The mighty oak honours the trust we place in it.
We must honour the faith placed in us by the
gods, and ensure that acorns, falling to earth
in our lifetime, produce a rich harvest for
those who come after us.

asc

æʃc biþ oƀenheah   eldum dÿne
ʃtiþ on ʃtaþule   ʃtede nihte hÿlt
ðeah him ƀeohtan on   ƀinaʃ moniᵹe.

Ash is very high and much valued by men.
Firm in the ground, it holds its place
and resists well the many attacks of men.

The ash grows quickly and, when cut back,
produces a fine crop. It makes a stout fence
for a settlement, a strong shield and a straight spear.

Ash is endurance, perseverance and determination.
It helps provide us with shelter and
protection from our foes.

yr

ẏn bẏþ æþelinʒa   an eonla ʒehþæf
þẏn anð þẏnþmẏnð   bẏþ on picʒe fæʒen
fæftlic on fænelde   fẏnðʒeatepa fum.

The axe-hammer is, for princes and for every warrior,
joy and an honour. It is fair on a horse;
dependable on the journey, part of warlike arms.

The axe-hammer is a fine
piece of war-gear with
which to break through
a shield-wall and hack
through a helmet. It
has many uses on a
journey and looks
splendid hanging
from a saddle.

ior

ıop bȳþ eaꝼıxa   anꝺ ꝺeah a bꞃuceþ
ꝼoꝺneſ on ꝼalꝺan   haꝼaþ ꝼægepne eapꝺ
þætpe bepoppen   ꝺæp he pȳnnum leoꝼaþ.

The beaver is a river fish, yet it always eats
its food on the ground. It has a fair home
surrounded by water where it dwells in contentment.

The beaver swims like a fish but eats bark and twigs.
It works hard to build a home where it lives in
happiness and contentment.

ear

 eaꞃ bẏþ eᵹle eoꞃla ᵹehᵹẏlcun
ꝺonn fæꞃꞇlice flæꞃc onᵹinneþ
hꞃaꝺ colian hꞃuꞃan ceoꞃan
blac ꞇo ᵹebeꝺꝺan blea ᵹeꝺꞃeoꞃaþ
pẏnna ᵹepiꞇaþ peꞃa ᵹeꞃpicaþ.

The grave is hateful to all men
when the flesh grows cold
and the pale corpse chooses the earth
as its companion. Riches fade;
joys pass away; friendships end.

Give thanks for life, the greatest of gifts,
and dwell not on the grave that awaits you.
We wrestle with old age in an unequal struggle from
the day we are born, but even the strong are humbled
by death. Let the certainty of an end to this life be a
spur to acts of courage and glory. Be bold, and your
fame will burn brightly in the minds of those you
leave behind and those who come after them.

The *Rune Poem* – edited text

feoh byþ frofur   fira gehwylcum
sceal ðeah manna gehwylc   miclun hyt dælan
gif he wile for drihtne   domes hleotan.

ur byþ anmod   and oferhyrned
felafrecne deor   feohteþ mid hornum
mære morstapa   þæt is modig wuht.

þorn byþ ðearle scearp   ðegna gehwylcum
anfeng ys yfyl   ungemetun reþe
manna gehwylcun   ðe him mid resteð.

os byþ ordfruma   ælcre spræce
wisdomes wraþu   and witena frofur
and eorla gehwam   eadnys and tohiht.

rad byþ on recyde   rinca gehwylcum
sefte and swiþhwæt   ðam ðe sitteþ onufan
meare mægenheardum   ofer milpaþas.

cen byþ cwicera gehwam   cuþ on fyre
blac and beorhtlic   byrneþ oftust
ðær hi æþelingas   inne restaþ.

gyfu gumena byþ   gleng and herenys
wraþu and wyrþscype   and wræcna gehwam
ar and ætwist   ðe byþ oþra leas.

wenne bruceþ   ðe can weana lyt
sares and forge   and him sylfa hæfþ
blæd and blysse   and eac byrga geniht.

hægl byþ hwitust corna   hwyrft hit of heofones lyfte
wealcaþ hit windes scura   weorþeþ hit to wætere syððan.

nyd byþ nearu on breostan   weorþeþ hi ðeah oft niþa bearnum
to helpe and to hæle gehwæþre   gif hi his hlystaþ æror.

is byþ oferceald   ungemetum slidor
glisnaþ glæshluttur   gimmum gelicust
flor forste geworuht   fæger ansyne.

ger byþ gumena hiht   ðon god læteþ
halig heofones cyning   hrusan syllan
beorhte bleda   beornum and ðearfum.

eoh byþ utan   unsmeþe treow
heard hrusan fæst   hyrde fyres
wyrtrumun underwreþyd   wynan on eþle.

peorð byþ symble   plega and hlehter
wlancum   ðar wigan sittaþ
on beorsele   bliþe ætsomne.

eolhxsecg eard hæfþ   oftust on fenne
wexeð on wature   wundaþ grimme
blode breneðþ   beorna gehwylcne
ðe him ænigne   onfeng gedeð

segel semannum   symble biþ on hihte
ðonn hi hine feriaþ   ofer fisces beþ
oþ hibrim hengest   bringeþ to lande.

Tiw biþ tacna sum   healdeþ trywa wel
wiþ æþelingas   a biþ on færylde
ofer nihta genipu   næfre swiceþ

beorc byþ bleda leas   bereþ efne swa ðeah
tanas butan tudder   biþ on telgum wlitig
þeah on helme   hrysted fægere
geloden leafum   lyfte getenge.

eh byþ for eorlum   æþelinga wyn
hors hofum wlanc   ðær him hæleþe ymb
welege on wicgum   wrixlaþ spræce
and biþ unstyllum   æfre frofur

man byþ on myrgþe   his magan leof
sceal þeah anra gehwylc   odrum swican
for ðam dryhten wyle   dome sine
þæt earme flæsc   eorþan betæcan.

lagu byþ leodum   langsum geþuht
gif hi sculun neþun   on nacan tealtum
and hi sæ yþa   swyþe bregaþ
and se brim hengest   bridles ne gym.

119

Ing wæs ærest   mid eastdenum
ge sewen secgun   oþ he siððan est
ofer wæg gewat   wæn æfter ran
ðus heardingas   ðone hæle nemdun

eþel byþ oferleof   æghwylcum men
gif he mot ðær rihtes   and gerysena on
brucan on bolde   bleadum oftast

dæg byþ drihtnes sond   deore mannum
mære metodes leoht   myrgþ and tohiht
eadgum and earmum   eallum brice

ac byþ on eorþan   elda bearnum
flæsces fodor   fereþ gelome
ofer ganotes bæþ   garsecg fandaþ
hwæþer ac hæbbe   æþele treowe.

æsc biþ oferheab   eldum dyre
stiþ on staþule   stede rihte hylt
ðeah him feohtan on   firas monige.

yr byþ æþelinga   and eorla gehwæs
wyn and wyrþmynd   byþ on wicge fæger
fæstlic on færelde   fyrdgeacewa sum.

ior byþ eafixa   and ðeah abruceþ
fodres onfaldan   hafaþ fægerne eard
wætre beworpen   ðær he wynnum leofaþ.

ear byþ egle   eorla gehwylcun
ðonn fæstlice   flæsc onginneþ
hraw colian   hrusan ceosan
blac to gebeddan   bleda gedreosaþ
wynna gewitaþ   wera geswicaþ.

Witches and Wizards

For reasons that are not clear, but which may be due to a reluctance to use the word 'witch', it has become customary to use 'wicca' (pronounced 'wicker') as a synonym for witchcraft. This usage seems strange as it is probable that most witches are women and 'wicca' is the masculine form of the Old English word for witch and should be pronounced 'wicha'. (In Old English 'cc' was pronounced 'ch', as in 'chase'). The meaning of the Old English word *wicce* (feminine) is, a witch, sorceress. The meaning of *wicca*, (masculine) is, a wizard, soothsayer, sorcerer, magician. The plural in both cases is *wiccan* (pronounced wichan). There is no evidence to suggest that 'witch' in either its masculine or feminine form derives from or means 'wise'. All that can be said with any certainty is that *wicca* meant, a wizard, sorcerer, soothsayer, and that *wicce* meant, witch, sorceress. Both forms of the word may be linked to Middle Low German *wicken,* 'to conjure', or to Swedish *vicka,* 'to move to and fro'.

Middle English 'wicche' was used for both men and women but Middle English 'wizard' (M.E. *wysard* − wise+ard) came into use about the 15th century and although it was not originally a gender specific term it came to be used as the term for a male witch. In more recent times 'wizard' has been linked with specialist areas of witchcraft such as ritual magic, and as a result some people feel uncomfortable using it as a general term. Indeed some see no need to differentiate between male and female witches and argue that there are just witches. That may be true, but it is useful to have a means of distinguishing one from the other (as the early English had) and to do so by constantly referring to male and female witches is hardly satisfactory.

'Warlock' is an Old English word, *wærloga*, which is 'truth-liar' or 'oath-liar' and means oath-breaker, liar, scoundrel, traitor. It may have been used by Christians as a term of abuse for wizards or it may have been used to describe a practitioner of 'black magic' as the word seems to be associated with the devil. Because it is an inappropriate word that carries a pejorative meaning, it is not really suitable for use here. For the same reason *hag* is not used for a female witch although it seems to be derived from the Old English word *hægtesse* or *hegtes*, meaning fury or witch.

In Modern English 'witch' can be used to describe both male and female practitioners of witchcraft, and that is the way most modern heathens use the term. It is by no means certain that this modern usage reflects the ancient usage and in an attempt to clarify matters, and to avoid using *wicca* and *wicce*, a female witch will be called a witch and a male witch will be called a wizard.

The New Witchcraft

One of the main differences between the old witchcraft and modern witchcraft is that the practitioners of the former had skills to offer society as a whole and were important members of that society. Some, but by no means all, modern 'Western' witches appear to have few, if any, skills that are useful to society. They tend to be inward looking and concerned primarily with their personal fulfilment and the study and collection of obscure information from alien cultures. This approach, which is probably often adopted because it is associated with 'high magic' and high status, can be defended on the grounds that an eclectic approach to witchcraft is preferred. Such an outlook is a reasonable one to hold but it does not explain why so many of those adopting that approach should choose to ignore information available from their own heritage. Few appear to have any interest in, or knowledge of, the beliefs and mythology that shaped the activities and perceptions of witches in Anglo-Saxon society. This is a pity as it is almost certain that the heathen religion of Northern Europe, with its symbols, myths and legends, played an important part in the beliefs and practices of many European witches. Perhaps the reason for this aversion is that witchcraft is sometimes used as a spiritual home for feminists and they associate the Northern Tradition with Vikings and the promotion of aggressive masculine values. Such a view is understandable but mistaken, as I hope this book will indicate.

Similar complaints can be made about many members of the modern 'pagan' and New Age movement, who tend to identify with the Celts, who they regard as ancient vegetarian hippies who lived in peace and harmony with the earth and each other. The Anglo-Saxons and Vikings on the other hand are perceived as having been nasty blood-thirsty barbarians with no culture worthy of mention or interest. Such ignorance! Witchcraft and heathenism are not what they used to be.

The Old Witchcraft

The word witchcraft (*wicce-cræft*) means sorcery, magic art, or simply the craft of witches. The Old English word *cræft* means power, art or skill. The wisdom, knowledge and skills possessed by witches and wizards, and the extent to which there was specialization between or among the sexes, is not known but if the limited amount of direct evidence is supplemented with information from other similar heathen societies it is possible to construct a rough speculative model.

Witchcraft covered a much wider range of skills than is popularly believed and may have included the following specialist areas:

1. Midwifery; (O.E. middewif);
2. Soothsaying; (including weather lore);
3. Wortcraft – herbalism (O.E. wyrt = herb, plant; cræft = power, art or skill);
4. Soulcraft (psychology and magic);
5. Lorecraft (wardens of the laws and rituals);
6. Starcraft (wardens of the calendar and festivals).

It is probable that witches and wizards in heathen English society possessed some degree of skill and knowledge in each of these specialist areas but witches tended mainly to practise the first two skills (midwifery and soothsaying) while wizards tended to specialize in the last two areas (lorecraft and starcraft). Wortcraft and soulcraft may have been a skill shared equally by both.

1. Midwifery

In heathen English society, as in other pre-modern societies, it was usual for women to care for other women during childbirth, and for various rituals to be performed before, during and after the birth. Some rituals may have involved administering potions to ease the delivery or aid recovery, while others were for the purpose of discovering what Wyrd had in store for the child. For example when Brutus was still in his mother's womb lots were cast to see what the future held for him.

> *Perceived were the facts that the woman was with child. Then sent Ascanius, who was lord and duke, for them throughout that land who knew the chant of sorcery. He wanted to know through the black arts what sort of being it was that the woman had in her womb. They cast their lots – the devil was in it all; they found by that skill doleful news, that the woman was carrying a son, who was to be a prodigy...... The lots were cast, and so it all turned out.*
>
> (Layamon's *Brut*, verses 266–280 Trans. Griffiths)

The following Old English charm is for the purpose of protecting a child against early death, and possibly against being miscarried. The aim is to remove harmful spirits from the woman so that they cannot enter her child while it is in her womb or while it is being fed from her breast.

The woman who cannot bring her child to maturity must go to the grave of a dead man, step three times over the grave and say these words three times:

This is my help against the evil late birth,
this is my help against the grievous dismal birth,
this is my help against the evil lame birth.

And when the woman is with child and she goes to bed with her husband then she must say:

Up I go, step over you
with a live child, not with a dying one,
with a full-born child, not with a doomed one.

And when the mother feels that the child is alive, she must go to church, and when she comes in front of the altar, then she must say:

Christ, I said, testify that it is true
Christ, I said, witness that it is true

The woman who cannot bring her child to maturity must take part of the grave of her own child, wrap it up in black wool and sell it to merchants. And then she must say:

I sell it, you must sell it,
this black wool and the seeds of this grief.

The woman who cannot bring her child to maturity must take the milk of a cow of one colour in her hand, sip up a little with her mouth, and then go to running water and spit the milk into it. And then with the same hand she must take a mouthful of water and swallow it. Let her then say these words:

Everywhere I carried with me this great strong one,
strong because of this great food;
such a one I want to have and go home with.

When she goes to the stream she must not look round, nor again when she goes away from there, and let her go into another house than the one she started, and there take food.

A possible explanation of the magical structure of this charm is that by stepping over the grave of a dead man the woman demonstrates that she is stronger than death and in doing so she drives the death-spirit out of her body.

When she is pregnant she steps over her husband three times and in doing so she helps protect her child by both reminding death of her power and by invoking her husband's life-spirit so that it can give her greater strength and help her defend the child. Months later the woman goes to the church to call on Christ (and presumably the priest) to witness and confirm the live child she can feel within her. This may have replaced an earlier heathen practice which involved visiting a shrine, perhaps to Frig, the Mother, or to Ing, the God of Fertility and symbol of change and new life.

Shortly before the expected birth the woman must cast out the sorrow she has for the loss of an earlier child. She does this by symbolically giving her grief, in the form of the earth from the grave and the black wool, to a merchant who will take it to an unknown place far away, from which it will be unable to return. By her actions she rejects and casts out the spirit of sorrow and prevents it from finding its way back to her.

Cows of one colour were probably very rare and their milk of special significance, perhaps because it was thought to be pure. When she takes the milk into her mouth, the harmful spirit within her, which had previously entered her child through her milk, enters the cows milk and is spat out into a running stream which carries it far away. The drink of running water has a purifying effect which destroys any remaining trace of the spirit. If by any chance the expelled spirit should escape from the stream it will be confused by her leaving along a different path and going to a different house. By not looking round she symbolizes the finality of the parting and it is, perhaps, meant to prevent the spirit from re-entering her body.

2. Soothsaying

A soothsayer is a truth-speaker (O.E. *soth*=truth), that is, a person who is able to discover unknown things or foretell future events by supernatural means. Women were regarded as having greater powers of prophecy than men and it is clear from Tacitus that it was women who were consulted when there was a need to know what the future held in store. Tacitus mentions in *Germania* that the Germans believed that there resided in women an element of holiness and a gift of prophecy. That view is supported in Caesar's *The Conquest of Gaul.*

> *When Caesar enquired of the captives why Ariovistus had not decided on battle, he obtained this explanation: that among the Germans it was the custom that the matrons of the tribe would, by means of lots and of divination, discover whether it would be advantageous to go to battle or not.*

(De Bello Gallico. Trans. Griffiths)

There is also evidence to show that the women involved in divination and the casting of lots were associated with runes, perhaps because they used runic symbols for divination or because they possessed secret and mysterious knowledge. Tacitus when speaking of the priestesses and prophetesses of the Germans, says; *"But once they also venerated Aurina and several other female beings, but not with servile adulation, nor so as to make of them goddesses."* Kemble suggests that Tacitus took *Aurina* to be the proper name of a woman whereas it was a general, or generic term, for a prophetess or sorceress, in short *Alrynia.* Kemble quotes a piece from Jornanthes, about Filimer expelling from his kingdom, *"certain female enchantresses, who in the native tongue they call Aliorunnae."* Aurina, Alrynia and Aliorunnae contain an early form of the word 'rune', and demonstrate a link between runes and priestesses, prophetesses, and enchantresses.

The evidence for men using runes during the early period may also be found with Tacitus (*Germania, 10*) who gives a good description of how one Germanic people cast lots during the 1st century.

> *Their procedure in casting lots is always the same. They cut a branch from a nut bearing tree and slice it into strips; these they mark with distinctive signs. The pieces of wood are then scattered at random on a white cloth. The head priest (if it is a public consultation) or the father of the family (if it is private) offers a prayer to the gods, and while looking up at the sky, picks up three sticks, and reads their meaning according to the signs cut on them. If an enterprise is forbidden by the lots, there is no deliberation on the matter in question that day. If the lots allow an enterprise, confirmation is sought by the taking of auspices.*

Two points arise from this passage. The first is that, although the 'distinctive signs' mentioned above are not called runes, it seems in all probability that they were, although they may not have been the runes of the Elder Futhark. The second point is that divination and the casting of lots are not necessarily the same thing and it is possible that women specialized in the former and men in the latter. Divination is concerned with seeking knowledge of the future by magical means whereas lots are usually used for the purpose of making a decision.

Instances of the casting of lots are recorded in several places but it is not always clear who conducted the ceremony.

> *He said that in his own presence an answer was sought three times concerning him by the casting of lots, whether he should immediately be killed by fire or held over until another time: by the lucky chance of the lots he survived.*

(De Bello Gallico. Trans. Griffiths)

For they still have no king, just as the old Saxons did not, but several governors put in power over their tribe; these, when a time of war occurs, all cast lots, and whoever the lot picks out, him they all follow as leader for the duration of the warfare and him they obey: but when the war is finished, they are each governors again of equal rank.

(Bede. *Hist. Eccl.* Trans. Griffiths)

Then was altogether in the public place the people collected. They let among them the twig decide, which of them first unto the others should, for a supply of food, his life give up. They cast lots with hellish craft before the heathen gods, they reckoned among themselves. Then went the twig even over one of the old comrades, who was a councillor to the power of the warriors, a leader in the host. Quickly was he then fast in fetters despairing of life.

(*Vercelli Codex.* Trans. Kemble)

The twig referred to in the last quotation may have been one of a bunch of twigs on which signs, possibly runes, were marked. The procedures may have involved those taking part drawing a twig from a container and holding it up for all to see. The person drawing the marked twig was the one to be sacrificed. Another possibility is that a rune wand or a divining rod was passed over the heads of those assembled and when it dipped, the person so selected became the sacrificial victim. Whatever the system used Kemble believed it to be clear from the circumstances that in none of these cases was a mere casting of lots intended He thought it obvious that they were auguries or divinations. However, it is difficult to understand why he should have been so convinced that the rituals where not 'merely' a casting of lots.

Another reference to the selection of a person for sacrifice appears in *Gautreks Saga* where a Viking, King Vikar, prayed to Woden asking for a favourable wind. Lots were drawn to see who should be sacrificed and Vikar himself was chosen. The king's companions suggested that a mock sacrifice would be enough to appease Woden and Vikar agreed to play his part. The king stood on a tree stump under the sturdy branch of a fir tree which had been bent down under the weight of many men and tied with a rope. A calf's intestines were looped round Vikar's neck and fastened to the branch above. The person conducting the ceremony stood before the king with a rod in his hand and spoke the words of dedication. 'Now I give you to Odin'. The ritual became reality and the rod became a spear which pierced the king's heart The intestine became a strong cord and when the stump was kicked away, and the rope was cut, Vikar's body was quickly jerked high into the tree where it was left to hang as a sacrifice to Odin.

Information about divination during the early English period is scarce but a few interesting graves of high-status women have been found containing three objects that were hung from a waistband. The objects, which are shown in the rune drawing for 'birch', are a crystal ball, a strainer and a pair of tweezers. Crystal has long been associated with the powers of prophecy, and a strainer and tweezers could have been used in the preparation of potions. The items may not have been functional but merely symbols of their owner's status or craft, in much the same way that latch-keys were worn hanging from a waistband and had, in addition to their functional use, the purpose of showing that the wearer was a householder.

Weathercraft

Weathercraft is a branch of soothsaying about which little can be said other than that it was based on observation and the application of general rules. Because of the great variation in local climate in England, weathercraft must have required careful observation and accurate record-keeping for weather patterns to be recognized. The general rules were probably committed to memory in much the same way as much other information in an oral society was, that is in the form of a rhyme. Perhaps a few of those rules have come down to us in the form of old wives' tales such as; 'Red sky at night shepherds' delight, red sky in the morning shepherds' warning'. It is probable that witches used basic information drawn from observation, and added that magical ingredient, intuition. As in other areas of their craft they were probably reasonably successful.

The extent to which local communities were dependent on the weather-forecasting skills of witches is impossible to say but it is unlikely to have been very great as they were primarily agricultural societies and most people in those times worked in the open and would have learned for themselves to 'read' the weather. The rhymes that contained the general rules were probably part of a folklore that has for the most part been lost.

An area of weathercraft exclusive to witches and wizards was the ability to change the weather for good or bad. There were obviously no penalties for bringing favourable weather but among a list of punishments for heathens recorded about 690 CE there is an entry which states;

> *Anyone who is a sender of storm, that is evil-doing, is to do seven years penance, three on bread and water.*

3. Wortcraft or Wortcunning

Knowledge about plants and their medicinal properties is probably one of the oldest skills possessed by mankind. Over tens of thousands of years of observation, and trial and error, a large body of knowledge was built up and passed on from generation to generation by word of mouth. Some simple remedies were probably widely known within societies but others were the jealously guarded secrets of specialists. Although such information would not have been given away it is likely that specialists exchanged information and in this way knowledge passed from one society to another. Differences in climate and vegetation gave rise to different illnesses and different remedies in different places but much of the information was of universal interest and probably entered a pool of common knowledge. Cultural differences would not have been an insurmountable barrier to the spread of information as the desire for greater knowledge, which was equated with status and power, was probably a powerful motivation, as was local professional rivalry. The practitioners of wortcraft in heathen England had access to much the same pool of information as other European peoples. It should not be assumed, as is often done, that those societies that first recorded the remedies were the originators or sole possessors of the information. Many herbal and other remedies were first recorded in Latin but that does not mean that the remedies were discovered by those societies. The transfer of knowledge was multi-directional and not, as is commonly thought, only northwards from the Mediterranean.

Many of the spells, curses, and potions known to the heathen English have survived and nearly all of them can be found in *Leechdoms, Wortcunning and Starcraft of Early England* (three volumes 1864-66), by the Rev. Oswald Cockayne, which contains a collection of assorted remedies that were known to the Anglo-Saxons, Romans and Greeks. The main source of information is a three-part Winchester manuscript dated about 950, the first two sections are known as Bald's *Leechbook,* and the third as *Leechbook III.* Another, later, source is *Lacnunga* (Remedies).

The potions and spells are mostly pre-Christian in origin but some have been added to or modified by the Christians who recorded them so as to remove references to heathen gods or to insert their own god. We can however reverse the process of censorship and get near to the probable, or possible, original heathen wording and meaning. Some of the charms are constructed in the traditional heathen manner but are entirely Christian in content and are sometimes written in Latin or Greek. In other words, the principles of magical theory have been applied but in a Christian context.

The remedies and charms include the following titles:

For a swarm of bees;
Against rheumatism;
Against a dwarf;
Against theft;
Against elf-sickness and elf-disease;
Against tumours;
Against elf-shot;
Against the devil and insanity;
Against witches and elvish tricks;
For a woman big with child;
If a horse has a sprained leg;
A remedy for your cattle;
Against tooth-ache;
To stanch bleeding;
If a woman cannot bear children;
To obtain favours.

The recipes have usually been treated by those studying them as a branch of magic rather than medicine, as did Dr. Storms in his book *Anglo-Saxon Magic.* Whatever the reason for the inclusion of the various ingredients in the potions it must be presumed that most of the remedies worked most of the time because if they had not, the healers would have lost their customers. It is improbable that people would have continued to seek the help of healers, and to have paid for the privilege of doing so, if they were never cured. This line of thought has been pursued in recent years and the prescriptions have been treated as medical documents. It has been shown that some of the remedies are rational, effective and based on observation and experiment. M. L. Cameron ('Anglo-Saxon Medicine and Magic', in *Anglo-Saxon England No.17*, and an excellent book, *Anglo-Saxon Medicine*, 1993) has examined some of the recipes in this way and explained why they were effective. He looked at a remedy which Storms had believed to be a piece of sympathetic magic (the theory of similarity); of which more later: *"For headache, hound's head, burn to ashes and shave the head, lay on."* Cameron argued that the remedy is rational and based on the knowledge that ash is a dessicant and known to dry up wet ulcers. (Much would seem to depend however on what is meant by 'headache'.)

Cameron looked at other remedies that had been described as magical but which can be shown to be rational: ' *"For distress of the stomach . . . . . rub pennyroyal in vinegar and water, give to drink, the pain goes away at once."* Pennyroyal is a carminative and used in modern medicine for its ability to relieve a distressed stomach.

> *Make an eyesalve for a wen: take cropleek and garlic equal amounts of both, pound well together, take equal amounts of wine and bull's gall and mix with the leeks, then put in a brass vessel, let stand for nine nights in the brass vessel, wring out through a cloth and clear well, put in a horn and about night time put on the eye with a feather. The best remedy.*

According to Storms, the main feature of mystification in this remedy was the use of a brass pot. Cameron interpreted it differently and suggested that the ailment (a stye on the eyelid) would most likely have been a staphylococcal infection of a hair follicle and that the ingredients of the salve would have been effective in treating it. Onion and garlic are antibiotics and garlic juice inhibits the growth of staphylococcus and several other kinds of bacterium. Bull's gall (oxgall) has detergent properties which make it effective against many bacterium, especially straphylococci, and enable it to dissolve the oily film on the eyelid, thus helping the potion penetrate to the site of the infection. The wine of that time, he suggests, would have contained acetic acid with which the copper in the brass would react to form copper salts which destroy bacterium. Keeping the mixture in the brass pot for nine days would have been sufficient time for the copper salts to form and its transfer to a neutral container would have helped preserve the mixture until it was needed. As Cameron points out it is improbable that someone seeking a remedy for an ailment such as a stye would be satisfied with a prescription that took nine days to be made up and it is likely that the healer would have kept various potions ready for dispensing to patients for immediate use.

The potion is very impressive because it is not just a general antibiotic, but one that contains ingredients that are particularly effective against the specific bacterium causing the infection. It can, perhaps, be concluded from this that the information contained in Bald's *Leechbook* was for the use of practitioners, and that the healers, whether witches, wizards or whatever, were not fools, and the knowledge they possessed enabled them to provide an effective remedy for many ailments. If they were unable to offer a salve or potion as a cure or a palliative, they employed psychology in conjunction with other means that can best be described as soulcraft or magic.

4. Soulcraft

The soul is the non-physical part of a person that includes personality, will, emotions, intellect, and spirituality. It is in effect the essence of a person and includes a person's mental faculties and perceptions. The soul, or perhaps the mind, is the thing that gives meaning to life, and soulcraft is an understanding of how to gain access to the inner core that makes each individual unique. The craft can be used to manipulate the mind and spirit of an individual for good or evil, and can be directed outwards to influence the way individuals perceive themselves and the world around them, or it can be directed inwards in a search for self-enlightenment and fulfilment.

Soulcraft was probably bound up with the belief that all objects, animate or inanimate, have souls and should be treated as such. A belief associated with this animistic outlook is that there is no division between the internal self and the external world, one merges into the other and everything is interlinked and interdependent. This does not, incidentally, mean that there is no conflict and competition in the universe. In the Northern Tradition conflict is an important and inescapable self-evident fact of life, and one that has to be faced. Nature is not a state of perfect harmony where there is no pain and suffering but one of conflict where many beings suffer an unpleasant life and death. To believe otherwise is unrealistic as, for example, contrary to what many like to think, the victims of carnivores do not necessarily enjoy painless, or even very quick deaths.

What is seen by some as harmony is in fact a balance of power between conflicting forces. This balance does not reflect an ideal state of affairs which has been constructed or planned but merely reflects the status quo at any given time. Some believe that long ago an ideal world existed (eg. the Garden of Eden) but others take the view that nature is an arbitrary and changing balance of forces. Nature is not static but in a continuous state of flux. There is no point in the evolution of the universe, or the Solar System, or the Earth that can be pinpointed as 'the natural state'. For example, is the natural, and presumably the ideal, state of Britain that where it is covered in forest and is uninhabited by people? Or perhaps it existed during the last Ice Age. These options will no doubt be looked on with favour by those who see mankind as unnatural or outside nature, and the cause of all the disharmony and suffering in this world. However, this view ignores the long period of the Earth's history before mankind evolved. That history is made up of many 'ages', that were each 'natural' for millions of years. Many of those periods ended in chaos when the stresses that were pulling them apart became stronger than those binding them together. Out of the chaos resulting from the collapse of one system came a new balance of forces that ushered in a new system.

The present system will come to an end just as those before it have and an understanding of this is built into the Norse branch of Germanic mythology. It foresees a time when the current system is overthrown by forces hostile to both mankind and the gods. In the final battle the gods will be defeated, and fire and smoke will rage across the Earth and lick heaven itself. The Sun will turn black and the land sink into the sea. When all has been destroyed by fire and flood the land will rise out of the sea and fields of corn will grow where none were sown. The sons of Odin (Woden) will survive and Balder (Ing) will return from Hel, the Realm of the Dead. A man and a woman will survive and from them will come a stock of people who will populate the whole Earth. Sun will bear a daughter who will follow the path of her mother.

Conflict was seen as having a positive as well as a negative side. A practical result of this outlook was the development of an enlightened self-interest in which individuals showed respect and consideration for other beings and things. Animals were still hunted and trees were cut down but the death of those living things was often an event to be accompanied by a ritual. The hunter who killed a stag or boar, or the person who ate certain parts of the animal, was thought to absorb some of the qualities of the beast. The person killing an animal or cutting down a tree would, in some instances at least, feel the need to appease the spirit of the animal or tree.

Shamanism

An aspect of soulcraft that can be dealt with here is shamanism, which is a branch of witchcraft that is mainly associated with wizards. The word 'shaman' is of Siberian origin but is used to describe a person from any society who seeks spiritual contact with other worlds and beings in a quest for enlightenment. Shamanism is an important part of the Northern tradition but it was, and is, practised in many cultures. Sometimes the quest is undertaken solely for the enlightenment of the shaman and on other occasions it might be for the benefit of someone who is sick and unable to make the journey themself.

Part of the shamanistic system of belief is the view that all individuals have, or can acquire, protective spirits. The shaman can travel to other worlds to find the guardian spirit of the sick person, or enter their body in order to combat harmful spirits or weapons. It was thought that ailments were sometimes caused by elves, goblins, and various spirits who attacked the body of the affected person by means of, for example, 'elf-shot', or 'elf-bolts', which were the invisible arrows and spears used by elves and goblins to pierce the skin of their victims. The holes made by the weapons allowed spirits to enter the body and cause sickness, while the arrows and spears attacked muscles, joints and other parts, causing damage and pain. The cure for some ailments involved a combat between the shaman and the spirits. The rituals performed sometimes symbolized the course of that combat. For example there is a charm to cure horses (and probably cattle) against elf-shot. The ailment may have been that suffered in spring when horses and cattle eat too much of the new grass and suffer from a painful build up of gas in their bellies.

If a horse is elf-shot, take a knife which has a handle made from the fallow horn of an ox, and has three brass nails in it.
Then mark a cross on the forehead of the horse, so that the blood flows from it; then, likewise, mark a cross on the back of the horse and on all limbs into which you can cut. Then take the left ear and pierce it in silence.

131

This you shall do: Take a rod and beat the horse on the back, then it is cured.
And then on the horn handle of the knife write these words:
Benedicite omnia opera domini dominum.
Whatever elf has possessed it, this will cure him.

Perhaps during the ritual (probably when the ear was pierced as that was considered to be an opening into the body) the shaman went into a trance and entered the animal to do combat with the harmful spirits and to drive them, and the spears and arrows, out through the cuts. The cross, a pre-Christian sign for the sun, was an important and powerful symbol for Christians and heathens alike and may have been seen as a means of preventing the re-entry of harmful forces through the hole in the skin.

Writing, *Benedicite omnia opera domini dominum,* on the handle is obviously a Christian addition which may have replaced something heathen written in runes, or perhaps it was included simply to give a heathen charm a Christian element.

Beating the animal caused it to leap around and gave the hostile spirit within an unpleasant experience which encouraged it to leave through the wounds. Its escape was assisted by the flow of blood which, it was believed, helped to draw out those spirits. It was this principle that underlay those cures for lunacy which involved beating or whipping the possessed person.

The following is another example of a charm against the weapons of a being, or beings, who are causing a person to feel pain.

With a sudden pain [a stitch or sudden twinge of pain?] – *feverfew and the red*
nettle that grows through a house, and plantain; boil in butter.

Loud they were, lo loud, when they rode over the mound,
they were fierce when they rode over the land.
Shield yourself now that you may survive their attack.
Out little spear, if you are in here.
I stood under linden-wood, under a light shield,
where the mighty women displayed their power,
and screaming they sent forth their spears.
I will send them back another
an arrow flying towards them.
Out little spear, if you are in there.
A smith sat forging a little knife

. . . .(missing line incomplete and meaningless)

Out little spear if you are in here.
Six smiths sat making war-spears.
Out spear, not in spear.
If there is a speck of iron in here,
the work of hags, it shall melt.
Whether you were shot in the skin, or shot in the flesh,
or shot in the blood, or shot in the bone,
or shot in a limb, may your life never be harmed.

If it were the shot of the Æsir, or the shot of elves,
or the shot of hags, I will help you now.
This is your cure for the shot of the Æsir, this for the shot of elves,
this for the shot of hags, I will help you.
Fly to the mountain top.
Be whole. May the Lord help you.

Then take the knife and wet it with the potion.

It is believed that the above consists of two charms (or parts of two charms) which have been mistakenly joined together. However, despite its apparently incomplete form it does give the flavour of such charms and reveals the struggle that takes place between the power of the healer, and the power of the being, or beings, who are the cause of the ailment. Presumably the healer, or exorcist, performed symbolic actions while reciting the words of the charm, but what they were we do not know.

According to Dr Storms, the healer is invoking the assistance of unnamed-named mythological figures to help drive out the pain caused by elves or the Æsir (the gods) or hags (witches). Dr Storms goes on to explain that the word used in the text for mound means 'a grave' or 'burial mound', and that the linking of the 'mighty women', who he thinks are witches, with the dead gives added stress to their ferocity because, *"black magic was often practised in graveyards, and evil power was to be gained from contact with the dead"*. It would seem more probable that the 'mighty women' are Valkyries, as they were choosers of the slain and rode with Woden in the search for lost souls. They were, like the Wyrd Sisters, the daughters of Night and they carried spears, whereas witches do not appear to have done so. Another charm (below), which is probably meant to prevent a swarm of bees being lost to the owner of the hive, mentions 'victorious women', another synonym for Valkyries. It is easy to see why a connection should be made between Valkyries and a fierce swarm of bees who select a victim for attack and then, after pursuing it, leave painful stings (spears) embedded in the victim's skin.

Take earth and throw it with your right hand under your right foot and say:

I catch it under my foot; I have found it.
Lo, earth can prevail against every creature,
and against malice and against neglect,
and against the mighty tongue of man.

And then throw sand over them when they swarm and say:

Settle, victorious women, sink down to earth.
Never fly wild to the wood.
Be as mindful of my welfare
as each man is of food and home.

Getting back to the charm against sudden pain, it is probable that some Christian tinkering has taken place as it is more likely that a heathen shaman would invoke the power of the gods and the Valkyries rather than oppose them. The third line of the charm seem to support this view as it appears to be a threat which is meant to scare the harmful spirit away.

The charm may have required the shaman to enter the spirit world (a trance) with these powerful forces in support. The charm describes what the shaman is seeing (visualizing) and doing as s/he enters the body of the victim and struggles with the harmful spirits and seeks to expel them and the weapons with which they are inflicting pain.

The shaman's quest for knowledge, understanding, and a vision of the future may have involved journeying along the roots and branches of the universal tree to the other worlds. The chosen destination and the rune, or combination of runes, used in the trance-inducing ritual, presumably determined the nature of the experience he had and the insights gained. The ultimate aim was probably to journey to Heaven and speak with the gods. Once a new destination had been reached the shaman would probably have been able to return there using his own skill but, if the original visit had been under the influence of a potion of some kind, the subsequent journeys may have been flash-backs. The journeying aspect of shamanism has been developed into 'pathworking', which can be interesting, enlightening and fun.

There are several means by which shaman could have induced the trance that enabled them to journey to different worlds and enter the bodies of other beings. The methods, which are known to many cultures, include self-hypnosis, fasting, drugs, pain, meditation or chanting, dancing and drumming. Any one method, or combination of methods, may have been used. Hypnosis both of the self and of others is a very old skill and one which was probably possessed by the witches and wizards of that time. Fasting can induce hallucinations and the North American Indians are believed to have used such a method to contact the spirit world. They also used a drug extracted from cacti to help them on their spiritual journey and in this they were not unique as the use of hallucinates for that purpose is common to most early societies and there are a surprisingly large number of plants from which suitable drugs can be extracted. English witches and wizards would have had sufficient skills in wortcraft to select and process the appropriate plants to produce potions which they may have taken themselves or have administered to others, for the purpose of undertaking a journey. The Greeks used poppies and the Germanic peoples probably used, among other things, mushrooms. It has been suggested that drugs were used to enable the apprentices of the shaman to start their spiritual quest and make them aware of the experience they were aiming for by means of a self-induced trance. Shaman were probably aware of the dangers associated with the repeated use of powerful drugs and probably aimed to achieve a self-induced journey. The primary reason for preferring a self-induced journey is that it allows a shaman to have greater control over the journey. A drug-induced trance can be chaotic and leave the traveller as a helpless spectator of images over which there is no control.

When pain is used for the purpose of entering a trance it is usually self-inflicted. Self-flagellation is something known to Christianity and may have been one of the methods used by shaman. The story of Woden hanging from the World Tree for nine days and nights was probably known to the English and has been compared to the crucifixion of Christ. In the case of Woden it is likely that it was the pain and hunger he had to endure that induced the trance which enabled him to journey into the spirit world and return with the wisdom of the runes. It is said that he sacrificed himself to himself, which may mean that he endured the pain suffered by those who had been sacrificed to him by being hung from a tree with a spear wound beneath their heart. There has been some argument as to where the story originated as there are many similarities between Woden's ordeal, and Christ's crucifixion. It has been suggested that the Old English poem *The Dream of the Rood,* believed to have been written in the ninth century, is either a Christianized version of the experience undergone by Woden, or a Christian poem that borrows imagery from the traditional heathen verses that also inspired the runic inscription on the Ruthwell Cross. The following translation of part of the poem should be sufficient to demonstrate that it could have been adapted from a heathen poem describing a shamanic vision of the ordeal of Woden.

Listen while I tell you about a most vivid dream that came to me in the night while mortals slept in their beds. It was as though I saw a wondrous tree spreading high in the sky spun with light. The bright beacon was covered in gold and gleaming jewels. Mankind and all creation gazed on the tree of victory. Yet beneath the gold I could see marks made by the attacks of wretched men and on its right side it had bled. I was filled with sorrow and fear at the wondrous sight. I saw the marvellous tree change its coverings and hues. At times it was drenched by blood and gore, at other times it was adorned with treasure. I gazed on the site for a long while until I heard the noble tree speak these words to me:

Long ago I was cut down at the forest's edge, and removed from my roots. Strong enemies seized me to make from me a gallows from which to hang their felons. Men carried me upon their shoulders and many of them set me up on a hill and fastened me there. And then I saw the Lord of mankind hasten eagerly to mount me. The earth shook but I did not bend or break but stood firm although I could have struck down all his foes. The young hero, who was almighty God, resolute and unflinching climbed upon the gallows, bold under the sight of many watching men, since he wished to redeem mankind. I trembled when the warrior embraced me.

There is little information concerning the activities of witches but it seems reasonable to suppose that they sought the same sort of shamanic experiences as wizards although, if they modelled their rituals on the behaviour of the Valkyries or Wyrd Sisters, they would probably have performed them in groups, and some of the ceremonies would have been performed beside a well, pool or spring which perhaps represented the Spring of Destiny. The rites may have involved calling down the Moon into the pool during a ceremony that involved chanting and dancing, and served the purpose of helping them to enter a trance-like state. Perhaps the glimmer of moonlight on the water assisted that process and enabled them to speak with the sisters, Wyrd, Metod and Sculd, and travel the threads of the Web of Wyrd. Certain wells and springs in England have long been regarded as special places and are associated with rituals of unknown origin which have been taken over by the Church. The original purpose of the ceremonies may have been to give thanks to the gods for the water supply which was so important to the community and to ask that it be kept pure and alive. However witches, and other heathens, are more likely to have used springs, wells and pools away from settlements as places of worship. That springs were used for such purposes is evident from, *Punishments for heathens and others who turn from the Church of God*, written about the year 690.

> *If any make or perform a vow at trees, or springs, or stones, or boundaries, or anywhere other than in the house of God, let him do penance for three years on bread and water. This is sacrilege or demonic. If any eat or drink there let him do penance for one year on bread and water.*

It is not known for certain which species of tree the early English regarded as representing the universal tree but the yew is a strong contender. It is an evergreen, which is appropriate for a tree that should represent eternal life, and is also one of the longest living. It bears a poisonous berry from which a hallucinatory substance may have been produced and it has been suggested that the yew at certain times gives off a scent that can be intoxicating to those who inhale it. However this is hearsay and the truth of the statement is not known but making a potion from yew berries is not to be recommended as they are very poisonous.

In England the yew is associated with Church graveyards, and it has been suggested that this association, which has no Christian connotations, is due to the fact that some churches stand on sites formerly occupied by heathen places of worship. Some of the trees growing in churchyards are known to be well in excess of one thousand years old and were probably standing before the English political elite were converted to Christianity.

If the yew was the sacred tree of the heathen English it is likely that witches and wizards in heathen England believed the yew rune symbolized spiritual travel and was the key that gave them access to the other worlds. It was, perhaps, the rune on which they meditated in order to induce the trance that sent them on their quest.

Psychology and Magic

Soulcraft is a skill that in its widest sense can be rational and irrational and is in effect a mixture of psychology and magic. It can be argued that soulcraft is merely another name for magic and that psychology is but one of a magician's tools. However, the aim here is to separate the scientific and unscientific elements of soulcraft. The unscientific element will be called magic.

Magic is unscientific and can be said to be irrational. However, if the unscientific theory and rules of magic are accepted as being true and valid as a matter of faith, then magic has an internal logic and rationality. It might be said that psychology is that part of magical practice and theory for which a scientific explanation has been found. It can be seen that the boundary between science and magic is not constant.

The use of psychology to achieve certain ends is considered to be rational and scientific if a scientific explanation can be offered for the relationship between cause and effect, or it can be proved in a scientific way that there is a link between the two events, even though that link cannot be explained. Recognition is given to the placebo effect, and faith-healing has been shown to be effective with certain types of illness. Hypnotism is an ancient skill that was used effectively long before anyone could attempt to explain it in scientific terms and it was probably a skill possessed by some witches and wizards, and may be linked to the term 'spellbound'. Using any of these means to effect a cure or provide a palliative could, depending on the circumstances, be regarded as rational.

A magical act is one where there is neither a scientific explanation for how it works nor scientific proof that a link exists between the magical act and the claimed effect. Both psychology and magic can be used by a person to affect the mind of another person, or persons, so as to alter their perception of reality and in doing so, affect their physical being. With psychology it is possible to establish, in a scientific way, a link between cause and effect; with magic it is not possible to establish that link. In addition to altering a state of consciousness magicians also claim to be able to affect physical things (animal, vegetable and mineral) and also spiritual or non-physical things in this and other worlds. The scope of magic is obviously much wider than psychology.

The definition of magic given in Chambers Dictionary is, *the art of producing marvellous results by compelling the aid of spirits, or by using the secret forces of nature, such as the power supposed to reside in certain objects as 'givers of life'; enchantment; sorcery; the art of producing illusions by sleight of hand; a secret or mysterious power over the imagination or will.*

Another way of looking at magic is to see it as the power of mind over matter or the ability of one person, or group of persons, to alter the perceptions or states of consciousness of another person, or persons, by willing it. Magic is also the art of affecting physical things in a desired way by willing it. In essence, it is the means by which a desired effect is obtained in an unscientific way.

The means by which the magical power is harnessed, invoked or deployed is a spell. The spell usually consists of spoken or written words (or symbols) which form part of a ceremony. The spoken and written words may be in a form used many times before or that adapted for the special requirements of a particular occasion. The nature of the gods, spirits or beings invoked will depend upon the purpose of the spell. It would obviously be more appropriate at certain times to invoke the fertility goddess Frig and her son Ing, and on other occasions to invoke the war gods Tiw and Woden.

The extent to which a spell might be considered rational (ie.scientific) is, as we have seen with the brass pot earlier, likely to vary from time to time and place to place. This is not to imply that because some potions have been found to have medicinal properties, given time all of them will be found to be equally efficacious. What it does mean is that instead of dismissing much of the ancient wisdom and knowledge as worthless, and the ancient practitioners of witchcraft as superstitious fools, we should give them the credit they deserve for having preserved and added to an ancient body of knowledge, and for having provided a valuable service. Much of the time they did not know why something worked but it is not necessary for a process to be understood for it to be effective. Modern doctors use treatments that are not fully understood but we do not think any less of them because of that. We judge healers by their ability to cure an illness or alleviate the symptoms. If we were able to travel back in time, we would discover how useful the skills of witches were, and how limited our own knowledge and survival skills are by comparison. In the event of a common illness we would most likely have to visit a witch or wizard for a remedy, and it would probably be effective.

Soothsaying is, in the scientific sense of the word, an irrational activity and it is difficult, if not impossible, to argue otherwise. A person either believes in that sort of thing or does not and no amount of argument will change the view of a believer or non-believer. However magic is not quite so simple because although a theory applied by a practitioner may be unscientific (e.g. similarity) the way in which it can sometimes work is scientific. The use of a spell or charm to increase the fertility of animals or the soil is most certainly unscientific, but a curse placed on someone who believes that magic works is scientific because it relies on psychology, which is a science of sorts, to make it work.

The Basic Principles of Magic

Once several unprovable or unscientific, theories are accepted as being valid or 'true', magic has an internal logic and rationality. Belief in the validity of those theories is in essence a matter of faith and as such beyond rational debate.

The idea that underpins magic is that everything in both the physical and spiritual universe is linked and related. The Web of Wyrd perhaps represents this mass of connections where everything has an effect, however slight and remote, on everything else. This part of magic which is philosophical (theological) and seeks to explain the meaning of life and the universe is called high magic and would appear to have much to do with mythology. It is from high magic that science is said to have developed. That part of magic which is based on empiricism (trial and error) and which aims to produce practical results is called low magic and is sometimes called sorcery. This is the stuff of spells and charms where certain actions produce certain results. If a comparison is made with Christianity then the theologians are involved in high magic while local priests are concerned with low magic. It is arguable that the methods employed in herbalism, by the low magicians, were rational and scientific.

The practice of low magic is, for the most part, based on two ideas or theories. The first is that it is possible to produce an effect by imitating it; this is called the theory of 'similarity' and is probably best known as sympathetic magic. The second theory is that two objects once connected are always linked and that what is done to one object will affect the other; this has come to be known as 'contagion'.

Similarity

The method by which wizards and witches attempt to attain their objective often takes the form of some sort of comparison, either in actions or in words, between two similar things that are in some way brought together, so that what happens to one of them will also happen to the other. The similarity may be in appearance, sound, meaning, or colour. For example, an Anglo-Saxon remedy for a hard tumour is to take some hard, dry beans and boil them without salt and mix with honey. The boiling of the beans makes them soft and it is expected that the tumour will likewise become soft. The honey in the mixture enables it to adhere to the tumour on which it is spread and in this way the two things are brought together and the magic act is complete. The act is symbolic and, because of that, the comparison between the two similar things need not be expressed in full. The symbolism is clear to all those involved and it is not necessary for outsiders to understand the process, indeed it might be considered beneficial that they do not.

A remedy for a fractured skull involved applying an ointment consisting mainly of crushed bones bound together with other ingredients. It was believed that when the mixture was applied to the injured head the fractured bones would be bound together, just as the crushed bones had been, and in addition the power from the bones in the ointment would be absorbed and aid the healing process. The similarity in appearance between the bones in the ointment and the injured part added to the healing process. Further examples from Cockayne's *Leechdoms, Wortcunning and Starcraft of Early England* are given below.

> *Against a headache a dog's head is burnt to ashes and laid on.*[O.E. *hundes heafod* (hounds head) is probably the name of a plant; possibly the 'snapdragon']

> *If a man's limb is cut off, so that the marrow comes out, boiled sheep's marrow should be laid on the wound.*

> *As a remedy against snake-bite a black snake is washed in holy water and the water is then given to drink .* [Heathen holy water was probably dew.]

The following two Anglo-Saxon curses illustrate how sympathetic magic can take a verbal or written form.

> *May you be consumed as coal upon the hearth,*
> *may you shrink as dung upon a wall,*
> *and may you dry up as water in a pail.*
> *May you become as small as a linseed grain,*
> *and much smaller than the hipbone of an itchmite,*
> *and may you become so small that you become nothing.*

> *May he quite perish, as wood is consumed by fire,*
> *may he be as fragile as a thistle,*
> *he who plans to drive away these cattle*
> *or to carry off these goods.*

It is probable that a ritual of some kind accompanied the recital or writing down of the charms as spells seem to have almost always required an accompanying act. The *Nine Herb Charm* lists the nine herbs to be used against poison and infection, and then gives details of their strengths and powers. The protective power of Woden is then invoked and reference is made to the occasion when he killed a poisonous snake, and asks that, just as he provided protection against the poison of a snake before, he should do so again. The power of Woden is directed against the snake and its poison by taking nine birch twigs and marking the first rune of each of the nine herb names one to each twig. Presumably, it was not necessary to actually strike a snake with the twigs (staves) as it was the reciting of the words and the marking of the twigs with runes that constituted the magical act. The charm ends as follows;

If any poison comes flying from the east,
or from the north, or from the south,
or from the west among the people.

Christ stood over disease of every kind.

I alone know a running stream,
and the nine adders should take heed of it.
May all the weeds at this time spring up,
the seas slip apart, all salt water,
when I blow this poison from you.

The line mentioning Christ is an addition which can be removed or Woden can be substituted for Christ.

Dr Storms' explanation (*Anglo-Saxon Magic*) of the magical structure of the charm is that after the magician has recounted the strengths of the herbs and warned of the power of Woden he threatens to cast the snakes, or the spirits that bear infection, into a stream which will carry them away to the sea where they will be swallowed up.

Magic did not cease to be practised when the Church gained power in England and set about suppressing the Old Ways. Christians did as they had done in other countries and suppressed worship of the gods and those heathen practices and customs that could not be assimilated into the new religion. Some customs and festivals celebrated important periods in the agricultural and solar year and would have been difficult to suppress. In such cases the festivals were modified or renamed to make them appear Christian. The usual method was to make them a saint's feast day or a celebration of an event in Christian mythology.

Many spells retained their heathen roots and structure but were modified to remove overt references to the old gods. Christian additions such as, *Benedicite omnia opera domini dominum*, were inserted either to replace a heathen invocation or simply to give the spell a Christian flavour. The Church has its own magic but its spells and invocations are called prayers. When church congregations sing hymns or offer prayers to their god they are often not only praising him but using the principle of sympathetic magic as a means of invoking his power to bring about some desired result. It might be to heal or protect someone, or to bring peace, or help the poor and starving, or to help themselves in some way. The prayers often make reference to an event recorded in the bible, perhaps an act performed by Jesus or some other biblical character. A parallel is drawn between what was done by that person in the past and what is wanted now. Two examples of such prayers should suffice.

O God, merciful Father, who, in the time of Elisha the prophet, did suddenly in Samaria turn great scarcity and dearth into plenty and cheapness; have mercy upon us, that we, who are now for our sins punished with like adversity, may likewise find a seasonable relief. Increase the fruits of the earth by your heavenly benediction; and grant that we, receiving your bountiful liberality, may use the same to your glory, the relief of those that are needy, and our own comfort; through Jesus Christ our Lord, Amen.

O Almighty God, who in your anger did send a plague upon your own people in the wilderness, for their obstinate rebellion against Moses and Aaron; and also, in the time of king David, did slay with the plague of Pestilence three-score and ten thousand, and yet remembering your mercy did save the rest; have pity upon us miserable sinners, who are now visited with great sickness and mortality; that like as you did then accept of an atonement, and did command the destroying Angel to cease from punishing, so it may please you to withdraw from us this plague and grievous sickness; through Jesus Christ our Lord, Amen.

It can be seen in other ways that Christianity is no stranger to magic. The three wise men of Christian folklore (for which there is no scriptural authority) were magicians (*magi*=magicians). The miracles performed by Jesus and the saints, and the exorcism of evil spirits from persons or places by means of prayers and ritual are forms of magic.

Runes and Similarity

Runes were probably used in rituals to invoke supernatural powers either by being marked onto an object used in the ritual, or by being used to write a charm. It is probable that runes were also used in the preparation of potions. A few examples will make this clear.

a. A ritual to obtain success of some kind will benefit from marking the sun rune, *sigel,* ᛋ on something that burns brightly (eg. holly or yew) and then setting light to it. The sun rune represents success and good fortune.

b. A sheaf of corn or a corn dolly can be used to symbolize Frig. To invoke her power for the purpose of helping a woman to become pregnant the rune of Frig, ᛝ , which means 'fruitful year', can be marked on a piece of birch wood which is then attached to a corn dolly and hung over the bed of the woman for nine nights. The Frig rune represents fertility and love, a corn dolly is an offering made to Frig for a good harvest, and birch is the tree of fertility

c. To bring fine crops to the land, a loaf of bread should be made from grain set aside from the last good harvest. Mark it with the sign of Frig, ᛝ and Ing, ᛜ and then bake it and bury it in the first furrow of the year to be ploughed. The plough is a phallic symbol and the ploughing of the earth symbolizes its penetration and fertilization; the loaf being the semen.

d. To help a warrior retain his courage in battle, the rune of Tiw, ᛏ the God of Courage, should be marked on his weapon, be it sword or gun.

e. To protect a possession against theft, a curse charm should be marked on it in runes, or the curse may be in the form of a spell.

f. To give a potion magical properties it should be mixed or stored in a vessel marked with runes. Runes specific to the purpose of the potion can be used, either being marked on the vessel or marked on an ingredient to be dissolved in the potion. For example mark the healing birch rune, ᛒ on the leaf of a herb or on a piece of garlic before it is crushed and put into the potion. Use rune staves or a rune wand to stir the potion. If the futhorc is marked on vessels (eg. cauldrons) in which the potions are mixed, it will impart beneficial powers. With the examples given here, it will be helpful if an invocation of the appropriate god accompanies the act of marking the rune.

Writing the futhorc, or individual runes, on objects had two main purposes. First to protect the object or its owner or, in the case of a vessel or container, to protect the contents. The main purposes of the curse charms seems to have been to protect possessions from theft. The second reason for marking the futhorc on objects was to give them magical powers or, in the case of a container or vessel, to give the contents magical powers.

It would appear that the complete futhorc was sometimes used as a charm and it can be found marked on objects for no apparent reason other than as decoration or to give them magical powers, e.g. the runes marked on the ninth century Thames scramasax. R. I. Page (*An Introduction to English Runes*) gives several examples where carefully made expensive objects have runes very roughly scratched or otherwise marked on them. Page suggests that the apparently casual way in which the runes were made, may indicate that the process of marking the object, and the ritual that surrounded it, constituted the magical act. The rune marked on the object indicated that the appropriate ritual had been performed.

There is evidence from Scandinavia that runes were used for purposes other than magic. After a fire in the town of Bergen, Norway, an archaeological dig unearthed hundreds of bone and wooden runic objects which revealed that at a comparatively late date runes were used for quite mundane things, such as to record the owner of an object or note payments or debts. They were also used for more personal matters connected with love, childbirth and personal relationships. The Bergen runes suggest that it was more than just a small priestly class that was rune-literate. There is also Scandinavian evidence for runic number magic but, as with much else from Scandinavia, it provides useful information that is not necessarily applicable to heathen England because it is from a later period, and from a different society.

English evidence for runes being used to send messages can be found in the Old English poem, *The Husband's Message* (Exeter Book), where the message from the husband is related to the wife by the piece of wood on which the message is inscribed "*. . he who engraved this wood bade me to ask you . . .*" The poem ends with reference to the runes *sun*, *riding*, *grave* (or *ocean*), *joy* and *man*. " *I join* ᚼ *with* ᚱ *and* ᛣ *and* ᛈ *and* ᛗ *to declare on oath . .*" The poem could be a heathen riddle or derived from a charm but it might equally be Christian. Whatever the origin it seems to indicate that the audience would have been familiar with the idea of writing a runic message on a piece of wood. In this instance the runes are used as words rather than letters.

Charms may have been written on objects for the purpose of protecting them during a delicate and time-consuming manufacturing process. For example, it would have been most irritating, when making a comb, to break the last tooth to be cut or sawn.

Funeral urns, which are usually very crude and may have been made by the bereaved or the wizard conducting the funeral ritual, were often marked with runes or other rune-like symbols which were made while the clay was still wet.

It is probable that in English heathen society runes were marked on objects for the purpose of,

    a. invoking supernatural powers;
    b. giving the object supernatural powers;
    c. protecting the object or its owner.

Runes were marked as ideograms, singly or in groups, or as letters for the purpose of writing charms. In early times runes were used by witches and wizards mainly for mystical purposes, but in Scandinavia towards the end of the heathen period their use was unrestricted and many people were able to read and write with them.

Contagion

The first part of the theory of contagion is that any two or more objects that have been connected in some way retain a connection even when they are parted. The strength of the connection will depend on the extent to which the objects were physically and emotionally bound together.

The second part of the theory is that, because of the magical link between the separated objects it is possible to affect one object by doing something to the other, linked, object. The power of the magic depends on the strength of the linkage which is determined, in part, by the number of contacts, their duration, and the emotional connection between the objects. For example, a wedding dress, although worn only once, would probably provide a stronger link with its owner than a pair of frequently worn shoes. As a rough guide, the various types of physical linkage are between a person and something that was, or is:

    a. biologically part of the person, e.g. fingernails, hair;
    b. of sentimental value to the person;
    c. worn by the person;
    d. in physical contact with the person (eg. a finger ring);
    e. owned by the person.

Location or place can provide powerful links and it might be found useful to conduct a ritual in a current or former home, or workplace, of the person. The place of birth will provide a powerful link. Within the home the individual will probably have a stronger link with the bedroom than the attic. The reason for this might simply be that there has been greater physical contact with the bedroom and its contents, and more time has been spent there. It is also likely that deeper emotions have been felt in the bedroom.

An example of the application of the theory of contagion that immediately springs to mind is the incorporation into voodoo dolls of items that were physically part of, or otherwise linked to, the person to be affected. Wax played a part in Anglo-Saxon magic and it is probable that it was used to make models into which various symbolic objects were placed.

The examples above have all given a connection between a person and a thing or place but there is no reason why the connection should not be between two inanimate objects.

Emotion and Sacrifice

The power that a magical act conjures up is also dependent upon the amount of emotion and sacrifice invested in the ritual. As we have seen earlier the spoils of war were usually offered as a gift to the gods and sometimes a human sacrifice was also made. Such sacrifices certainly invested emotional content into the ritual, especially when lots were cast to determine who from among the warriors, including the leader, was to be sacrificed. The destruction, after a battle, of the valuable weapons, horses and other items captured from the enemy, was also a very great sacrifice.

The cost of a sacrifice, in emotional or financial terms, to an individual or group, determines to some extent the magical power generated by the sacrifice. However a sacrifice is not essential and emotion may be generated through ritual chanting, dancing or meditation. Emotive content is also related to the depth of commitment and belief that the practitioner puts into the magical act and the extent to which the desired result is wanted. Perhaps the experience and previous success of the magician is also a factor.

The point being made is that magic is not a mechanical thing that merely requires the performance of a ritual. It requires the investment of emotional energy (the willing of something to happen) and often involves paying a price.

Antiquity

Another factor of importance is the antiquity of the various elements that make up the rituals. If a ritual is required for a purpose for which there is no precedent, a new ritual can be created by adapting an old one or by amalgamating bits of several old rituals. Almost any ritual can be improved by including an appropriate rune. The power of runes is believed to be due in part to their antiquity and the long association between the symbol, name and idea. Their power is further enhanced if there is an ancestral link. For example English people (Anglo-Saxons) gain greater inspiration and power from Anglo-Saxon runes through the act of sharing an experience with their ancestors. In a similar way a place of worship, such as an ancient stone circle, gains power from its age and past use. Such places gain power from the magical and emotional investment that has been put into them.

White and Black Magic

The popular modern perception of magical practices is that there is white magic and black magic, with the former being used for the purpose of achieving a 'good' or beneficial objective, and the latter being used to promote 'evil', or harm to others. This idea is extended to witches who are likewise categorized as being 'white' or 'black'. Such perceptions do not reflect the reality of modern witchcraft or, what is more important to us here, the beliefs of those who practised the Old Ways in heathen England. Magic was probably regarded then, as it is now, as being neutral; a means to an end which could be used in the hope, or expectation, of achieving positive or negative results, just as chemistry and physics can. If that is borne in mind, 'white' and 'black, or 'positive' and 'negative', can be used to describe the purpose of the magic rather than the acts and principles involved, which are neutral regardless of the purpose to which they are put. When magic is used defensively it is not always easy to decide what is positive and what is negative. For example some Anglo-Saxon curses are defensive in that they are for the purpose of protecting cattle against theft, but they might be considered negative in that they seek the destruction of the thief. Where magic is used in an active form, for example when it is employed in a defensive pre-emptive manner to neutralize or destroy an enemy (ie. attack before being attacked), is it to be classified as positive or negative magic?

A deterrent to the use of negative magic is said to be, 'The Threefold Rule', which states that if you use magic to inflict harm on others it will come back to inflict threefold the harm on you. This is probably a modern 'rule', or at least one not known in Northern Europe where, so it seems, it was common to use magic to harm enemies and thieves. If there was such a rule then presumably there were exceptions to allow for the use of negative magic in time of war when each side employed all the resources at its disposal to obtain victory. Perhaps the cost of employing magic was not the harm suffered due to a rebound effect but, instead, the price that had to be paid, in the form of a sacrifice, to invoke the powers of the gods. The principle being that the greater the need for help the greater the price to be paid. Or, possibly, the rule was suspended in times of conflict and, just as Christian and other priests suspend adherence to what would appear to be an absolute rule, 'thou shall not kill', and are employed in wartime to lift the morale of soldiers who are about to kill as many of the enemy as they can, so the wizards of the Germanic tribes performed various magical ceremonies before a battle to improve the morale of their warriors and bring harm to the enemy, without incurring any magical penalty.

One form of magic involved the marking of runes on weapons. For example, the rune of Tiw was used to invoke his powers of courage and determination, while the rune of Woden, *os*, was marked on a spear that was thrown over the heads of the enemy before battle commenced. The magical effect of this, and other acts, was to make the limbs of the enemy feel tired and heavy so that they were unable to fight effectively. Another way to invoke magical powers was to wear, usually on a helmet, an image of a boar, an animal associated with courage, ferocity and tenacity in battle, as on the seventh-century Benty Grange helmet. (The boar is also a symbol of Ing.)

The belief that the powers, spirits or qualities of animals could be transferred to those who killed them, probably played some part in determining how they were sacrificed and by whom. Even the process of hunting and killing an animal, especially a powerful one, had symbolic significance and could be a spiritual experience in which the hunters absorbed the strengths of their prey. The wearing of the horns and skins of animals, such as the elk, bear or wolf, was also thought to invoke, or transfer to the wearer, some of the qualities possessed by the animal. The images we have of figures wearing brimmed hats with large decorated horns attached are probably those of wizards but they may have helped give rise to the belief that warriors had horns attached to their helmets. Such large stag or elk horns on a helmet would have been a great handicap in a battle. The Sutton Hoo helmet had no such attachments but part of its adornment depicts a horned figure. The Swedish Torslunda Bronze die shows a figure wearing the head of a bear or wolf.

Wizards would have used any magic that they thought necessary to give strength to their own side and to undermine that of the enemy. Whether the magic used was thought of as positive or negative may have depended on who was using it, the aggressor or the defender. Perhaps considerations of aggression and defence were not factors in deciding what was deemed good or bad in those distant times.

The campaign waged by the Church to suppress the Old Ways was likely to have been regarded by heathens as an act of war and a struggle for survival. Magic was one of the few weapons they had with which to fight and they would have used positive and negative magic as deemed necessary.

Christianity and Black Magic

The heathen English had a view of creation in which the qualities and powers of the Sky Father, in all his many manifestations, were complementary to the qualities and powers of Night and her many daughters. Christianity sought to replace those native gods with an all-powerful male god, and the history, values and outlook of an alien people. The Church called the heathen gods devils, and those who continued to worship them became, by definition, devil worshippers, and their magic was called black magic; black being equated with evil. Presumably Christian magic was thought of as white magic. The pools, wooden pillars, runes, rites and rituals of the followers of the Old Ways were linked with the devil (Satan, Lucifer) and, much later, when Christianity was in turmoil and obsessed by heresy, the Church waged a campaign of terror in which those who were thought to harbour beliefs incompatible with Christianity were at risk of being tortured and murdered. However, the extent and degree of persecution of heathens, and Christians, that took place in later times, does not seem to have occured in England prior to the Norman invasion.

Just as elves have no place in Christianity so the devil has no place in the Old Ways.

5. Lorecraft

It is apparent from the early reports of Tacitus and Caesar, and from English evidence, that men conducted public ceremonies and that those attending moots and the witan were men. The Witan, (O.E. *witan*, the plural of *wita* 'wise man') was the name given to the group of individuals selected to advise the king. During the Christian period it was made up of clergymen and important laymen. The representatives of the Church probably took the places previously reserved for wizards. Early Continental evidence suggests that kings were either made honorary wizards or selected from among them, and it seems that kings had at least one wizard to advise them.

In an oral society it was necessary to have many people responsible for the task of retaining and passing on the civil and criminal laws and customs. Tacitus (*Germania* 12) mentions magistrates being appointed by the moot for the purpose of administering justice in the districts and each one having one hundred advisers to assist him. One of the tasks of those advisors may have been, as mentioned earlier, to remember the decisions, sentences and awards of the courts. The early English administrative district called the 'hundred' may have its origins in that custom but it seems more probable that the name simply refers to the one hundred hides that made up a hundred. (A hide was the amount of land needed to support one family farmstead. The size of a hide and a hundred varied from one part of the country to another due, in part, to the fact that in some places the land was good for farming and, as a consequence, a family unit could exist on a smaller area of land than where it was bad. In some areas forty acres were enough for a farmstead while in others one hundred and twenty acres might be needed.)

Civil and religious rites and duties are often interlinked and bound together in early societies, and priests tended to serve as keepers of the laws. In heathen England, it is likely that wizards were either magistrates or legal advisers to magistrates. In the latter case they would have performed a function similar to that of a modern Clerk of the Court who gives advice on legal and procedural matters.

The keeping of laws and the observance of religious rites were combined in the ritual of beating the bounds, which still takes place in some parts of England during the Spring, often on May Day. It originally served the function of reminding the population as to where various boundaries lay. Early English legal documents reveal that boundaries were often described in terms that related them to landmarks such as trees, streams, and stones. Some boundaries were walked every year but others such as the Hundred or, later, parish boundaries were walked every second or more years and may have taken a day or more to complete. As the group, led by the wizard, walked they beat the ground with long willow wands, special attention being given to marker stones and trees where it became traditional for various activities such as 'bumping', or perhaps a beating, to take place. The purpose of these actions was to instil in the memories of those taking part the route that had been taken and the relevant land marks. It also reminded landowners where their boundaries lay. This regular demarcation of boundaries served to help prevent disputes and to enable those that did arise to be settled with the help of witnesses who had taken part in the ceremony. The second function of beating the earth was probably to awaken Ing, the Green Man, so that he might bring lush greenery to the fields and trees. At certain points on the walk the wizard cast a spell to improve the land just as a priest now says a prayer.

6. Starcraft

Starcraft overlaps with the other specialist areas, especially laws and rituals, and cannot be entirely separated from them. Starcraft was essentially the skill of keeping a calendar for the purpose of fixing the days on which moots and festivals were to be held. It is thought that moots were held about the time of the new moon or just after the full moon. New Year Day began four days after the Winter solstice and Mid-Summer day four days after the summer solstice.

We have various pieces of information about how the heathen English measured time but we cannot say, with any certainty, what the overall system was, although it is probable that it was a combination of lunar months and solar years. We know that time was measured in nights, months and years. A fortnight meant fourteen nights (O.E. *feorwertyne niht*) and days were measured from one sunset to the next. The word 'moon' comes from the Old English *mona*, and 'month' is from the Old English *monað*, meaning the period from one 'moon' to the next. That the heathen English used the month as a measure of time is evident from Bede's, *De Temporum Ratione*, written in 725, in which we also learn that the new year began on Midwinter Day (25th December, that is the night of the 24th/25th December). On the following night, Mothers' Night, certain ceremonies took place but we do not know what they were, although it seems reasonable to suppose that it was a time to give praise to the Earth Mother, Nerthus (or Frig), and to her son Ing, the God of Brightness. Perhaps it was a more meaningful Mothers Day than the one we have now. Kathleen Herbert (*Looking for the Lost Gods of England*) has suggested that the celebration may have been for the birth, to Frig (Nerthus), of Ing, the God of Brightness, with whom the turning of the year is associated. The symbol of Ing is the boar, and a boar's head is traditionally served on a bed of greenery on Midwinter Day, which is also Christmas Day. If the Night of Mothers was a celebration of the Mother of Creation and her giving birth to Ing, it would explain why the Church chose to celebrate the birth of Christ on that day and it would suggest that similar celebrations took place elsewhere in Europe before the introduction of Christianity.

The festivities, which went on for twelve nights (hence Twelfth Night), may have celebrated a different deity each day and involved taking meals with family and friends. Offering someone a place at your table is a greater, and more sincere, form of generosity than offering them a gift.

The last and first months of the year were called *Before Yule* and *After Yule* (O.E. *Ær Geol* and *Æfter Geol* – in Old English 'ge' is pronounced like modern 'y'). The meaning of the word Yule is unknown but it has been suggested that it has something to do with a wheel or circle, i.e. the turning of the year. It would appear that the fourth day after each solstice and equinox was a festival. Perhaps a lapse of four days was allowed to ensure, from observation, that the passage from one part of the year to the next had been accurately calculated and also to make some provision for the sun being hidden on cloudy days. Another explanation is that the four-day gap allowed time for those who wished to travel to the moot, festival, or other event to make the journey and camp there, or find accommodation.

The solar year system does not require precise calculation as to when it starts or ends as it relies ultimately on observation and is self-adjusting. The height of the sun in the sky was measured by the length of shadow cast by a sun dial which consisted of a pole of a given length. For example it is recorded that the shadow cast by a six-foot pole (at a certain location) at midday on 25th December was twenty-four feet while the entry for the 24th June was four feet. Measurements are also given for nine o'clock in the morning and three o'clock in the afternoon. Although all the measurements given are only in feet and half feet, those taking them would almost certainly have been far more accurate in their measurements and their records would have allowed them to calculate the solstices and equinoxes with some precision. Actual measurement of the shadow allowed them to adjust their imperfect calculations from time to time. Measurement by this means was quite sophisticated and it was known that the length of shadow cast by a pole of given length changed as it was moved further north or south.

The months of the year were as follows: (In O. E. ð and þ are pronounced 'th'; *g*, as used below, sounds like 'y', in year; æ as 'a' in ash)

1. *Æftera Geol* (Jan.): the month after Yule; the first month of the year.
2. *Solmonaþ*(Feb.): mud-month, the month when ceremonies involving the offering of cakes or loaves of bread to the Earth were held. Rituals involved the preparation of ploughs for the cutting of the first furrow. Part of one charm for a field ceremony involved boring a hole in the tail of the plough and putting incense, fennel, hallowed soap, and hallowed salt in it. Seed was then put on the body of the plough and a plea made to the Mother of Earth to grant a good crop. (see page 16) These field ceremonies probably took place on the first Monday after Twelfth Night (i.e. Plough Monday). The ploughing of a special loaf of bread or a cake into the first furrow made by the plough represented the impregnation and fertilization of the earth. Both Frig (Nerthus), the Earth Mother, and Allfather, the Sky Father, would have been worshipped at this time with their union being seen as necessary to bring fertility to the earth. In some parts of England this fertility ceremony was taken over by the Church and is now referred to as blessing the plough.
3. *Hreðmonaþ* (Mar.): month named after the goddess Hretha? Kathleen Herbert, *Looking for the Lost Gods of England*, points out that, "*Hreth* means 'glory, fame, triumph, honour', particularly as gained from military exploits. As an adjective, *hreðe* means 'fierce, cruel, rough', words that can describe the March winds as well as warriors. Hreð was a waelcyrie [valkyrie]; her month the last of winter." Birds start laying eggs in March and this, and the ancient association between eggs and fertility, gave rise to festivals connected with eggs (Shrove Tuesday – pancake day).
4. *Eostremonaþ* (Apr.): month named after the goddess Eostre (Easter) who could have been the companion of Ing, the Green Man. Eostre perhaps has some connection with the east and the rising sun. Kathleen Herbert suggests that Easter-month (Spring Equinox) marks the dawning of a new summer just as a sunrise marks the beginning of a new day.
5. *Þrimilce* (May): (Three-milkings) cows in milk and being milked three times daily.
6. *Ærra Liða* (June): Before Litha. The meaning of Litha is uncertain although 'moon' and 'calm' have been suggested. Bede gave the name 'Sailing-month' but Litha is probably either the name of a deity which guides the moon or the name for a power exerted by the moon. Perhaps the night of either the New Moon or Full Moon during the month preceding and following midsummer was sacred. The summer solstice was probably celebrated by lighting bonfires on hilltops. The festival may have begun on midsummer eve and continued for four days with the 'official' midsummer celebration starting, like midwinter, on the fourth day after the solstice.

7. *Æftera liða*: means After Litha – see above;
8. *Weodmonaþ*: month when weeds are prolific. Also the month in which special loaves are baked in celebration of the new grain harvest. The first day of Holy-month was probably the day in which a festival involving the baking and eating of bread from the new harvest took place. Perhaps some of the grain was 'blessed', with half being used immediately and the remainder stored away to bake loaves or cakes for the Plough Monday ceremony.;
9. *Haligmonaþ*: holy month, harvest-tide, month of offerings and thanks to Frig and the other Gods. A time for the harvest festival when produce from the harvest was given to the Gods; probably by being left in a temple or in the enclosure surrounding it. Enclosures were also made around stones, wells, trees and springs, and they too may have been places where sacrifices (tributes to the Gods) were left or where food and drink were taken by the participants to be consumed in a thanksgiving meal.
10. *Winterfylleþ*: winter begins with the first full moon of this month.
11. *Blotmonaþ*: month of blood when the animals that could not be kept over winter because of limited amounts of winter feed, were slaughtered and the meat salted, pickled or smoked. Some of the meat was roasted and a feast held to celebrate the occasion. The origin of bonfire night, which is celebrated throughout England on 5th November, is unknown but it is possible that it survives from the time when bones of the slaughtered animals were burnt to give thanks to the gods. (Bonfire was originally bone-fire);
12. *Geol*: the first part of Geol may have ended with the winter solstice and the second part began on Midwinter Day. The Festival of the Sun may have started twelve nights before Midwinter and was probably a Festival of Light involving fires.

We do not know how many days they had in a week (possibly five) or whether the number of months in a year varied (possibly twelve and thirteen), but many suggestions have been made as to how their calendar worked and how the lunar months and solar years were reconciled and incorporated into it.

As the lunar year of twelve months is about eleven days short of the solar year and a thirteen month lunar year about nineteen days longer it has been suggested that they used an eight year cycle as the basis of a lunar-solar calendar. If there were five years of twelve lunar months and three years of thirteen lunar months, the end of the lunar and solar years would very nearly coincide every eighth year. (Lunar month = 29.5306 days and a solar year = 365.2431 days) The extra, or thirteenth, month could have been an additional Litha.

Perhaps the lunar and solar systems were completely separate, with civic occasions, such as the moots, which were held around the time of either the new or full moon, being determined by the moon cycle, while religious festivals followed the sun cycle. It is probably partly the modern need to make things neat and tidy that gives rise to the idea that the two systems should be amalgamated.

Because festivals were an important part of life, it must have been the responsibility of a person or group to determine when they took place and how they were conducted. Until comparatively recent times, in western societies, it has been the prerogative of the Church to decide on matters relating to the calendar and it was almost certainly the guardians of the Old Ways who had that power in heathen England.

Summary

If there was specialization and a division of labour between witches and wizards, along the lines suggested above, the result would have been witches being more concerned with low magic (sorcery) and having greater contact than wizards with the ordinary people of the communities they served. The relationship of a witch with her neighbours was both professional and social. She was an important part of the local community whereas wizards were, for the most part, involved in high magic (theology/mythology) and the administration of the wider community, and acted as:

   a. members of the Witan and personal advisers to kings;
   b. officials who took part in the moot and the administration of justice;
   c. keepers of the calender and fesivals, and supervisors at funerals and public acts of worship;
   d the keeper of boundaries.

A witch attending a childbirth would have used her skills as a midwife, magician and herbalist, and the people attending would not have differentiated one element from another. Witchcraft was made up of many skills each of which gave support to the others so that the whole was greater than the sum of the parts. The mix of rational and irrational elements employed in any given instance would depend on the ability of the witch to directly influence events and obtain the desired result. For example, the remedy for a stye on the eyelid is, as we have seen, entirely rational and a most effective cure. The charm against the theft of cattle and other property employs psychology and is less certain because to be successful the potential thief has to know about the curse and believe that it will work. Spells and rituals, including the Christian prayers, which invoke the assistance of the gods, or god, and ask for relief from famine and sickness are pure magic as they are entirely unscientific and, a sceptic might say, can hope to do nothing except bring comfort to those who take part in them.

When a ritual has a high 'pure magic' content, it often has to be performed by someone other than the witch. For example, the Christianized heathen charm for unfruitful land which starts as follows.

For a person who wishes to improve their fields if crops will not grow properly or if any harm has been done to them by sorcery or witchcraft.

At night, before daybreak, take four sods from four sides of the land and mark how they stood. Then take oil and honey and yeast and milk of all the cattle that are on the land, and part of every tree growing on the land, except hard trees, and part of every well-known herb, except burdock, and pour holy water on them, and then let it drip three times on the bottom of the sods. Then say these words:

'Grow and multiply and fill the earth. In nominee patris et fillii et spiritus sancti sitis benedicti.'

151

And Our Father as often as the other. Afterwards carry the sods to church and have a priest sing four masses over them, and turn the green sides to the altar. Afterwards take the sods back to where they stood, before the setting sun.

To comply with all the requirements of this ritual would be quite a task. The possibility of failing to collect every necessary ingredient must have been extremely high. A cynic might suggest that witches and priests were expected to have a remedy for every ailment (just as modern doctors are) and they would have been reluctant to admit that they did not have a solution for every problem (just as modern doctors are). When they were asked to remedy something that was completely beyond their control they produced a ritual that was so complex and demanding that it would deter all but the most desperate. When the desired effect did not materialize the failure could be put down to the person who performed the ritual. Could they be absolutely certain that they had included all of the ingredients? Were only three drops of the potion dripped on to the bottom of the sods? Did they say the spell properly? If the person who performed the ritual could be certain in their own mind that they had done everything correctly, they were faced with the possibility that evil spirits were responsible for the failure.

The values and outlook on life engendered by English heathenism, and its variants practised elsewhere in the British Isles and Europe, in those distant times, have much in them that is attractive to many people today. The problem is that those who are drawn to heathen values and morality often regard the heathen past as a golden age when peace and goodwill reigned and mankind lived in harmony with nature. Sadly it is difficult to find evidence of such a golden age. It is also probable that many of the practices and beliefs of those times, such as whipping lunatics, would be completely unacceptable to most of today's heathens if they knew of them. Many people would also find the level of superstition, and the fear of harmful spirits and the magical powers of others, to be oppressive. It appears from the nature of many of the charms that individuals often sought protection from those who were using magic to harm or intimidate others.

Trial by ordeal was also a heathen practice which, in England, involved carrying a red hot iron bar for a given number of paces, or plunging a hand into boiling water to retrieve a stone. The number of paces, and the depth of the water, depended upon the gravity of the alleged offence. The theory behind this system of determining innocence or guilt, when other methods had failed, was probably based on the belief that the gods would heal the wounds of the innocent (within a given time limit). Such trials continued to take place after Christianity was introduced.

Some of these 'unacceptable' magical practices are still adhered to and recently, according to a newspaper report, two Moslem holy men have been jailed, "for killing a twenty-year-old woman during a ritual exorcism. The woman died after eight days of violence during which she was deprived of sleep and food, and beaten with sticks. A Home Office pathologist told the court that her injuries were consistent with her being jumped and stamped on. The 'holy men' apparently told the girl's mother that it was the evil spirit, not her daughter, who was suffering."

The Introduction of Christianity into England

From the arrival, in Kent, of Augustine in 597 Christianity gradually became the 'official' religion of the English kingdoms. English kings, and the challengers to their thrones, came increasingly to see the benefits to themselves of adopting Christianity and thereby gaining the backing of the Church with its national, and international, power and influence. Ethelbert the king of Kent was the first to submit to the Church, largely as a result of the influence of his wife Bertha, daughter of Charibert, a Christian king of the Franks. By adopting Christianity and recognising the Christian god as the one true god, and the Church as his mission on earth, and by allowing priests to go among his people, Ethelbert gained recognition from the Church and its allies as being the legitimate earthly ruler of the people of his kingdom.

As we have seen, it is probable that many wizards had a considerable amount of power and influence in heathen English society and they naturally wished to retain it. When the King seemed certain to convert, they could either oppose it, and face the prospect of redundancy, or denounce the Old Ways and become enthusiastic supporters of Christianity. Bede (*A History of the English Church and People*) records how Edwin, king of Northumbria wished to marry a daughter of Ethelbert, the king of Kent. Messengers were sent to Kent to request the hand of the princess in marriage but they were told that a Christian maiden could not be given in marriage to a heathen husband lest the Christian faith be profaned by her association with a king who was ignorant of the worship of the true god. Edwin replied that he would give the princess and her attendants, servants, and priests complete freedom to live and worship as they pleased. He also agreed to convert to Christianity if, after examination, he and his advisers thought it a better religion than their own. On this understanding the betrothal was agreed and Paulinus was consecrated as bishop so that he could accompany the princess and protect her and her companions from corruption by association with heathens. As soon as Paulinus arrived in Northumbria he set about trying to convert the people to Christianity but though he laboured long it was without success. Paulinus decided that it would be better to convert King Edwin so that his companions and the royal court would be obliged to follow. Once that was achieved clergymen would take the place of wizards as the King's advisers and be in a better position to convert the people.

When Edwin survived an assassination attempt and the Queen had the safe and painless delivery of a baby girl, the King gave thanks to the gods. Paulinus claimed both outcomes to be due to the power of Christ. Edwin said that if Christ would grant him life and victory over the king who had sent the assassin, he would renounce his gods and serve Christ. As a pledge that he would keep his word he agreed to have his daughter baptised. Edwin fought the West Saxons and was victorious but when he returned home he insisted that he and his advisers should consider the matter. About that time the King received a message, accompanied by a gift of a cloak and a tunic with a gold ornament, from Pope Boniface. Edwin was informed that the Christian god was worshipped by many people all over the earth and it was by him that kingship was conferred. Edwin was also told that the king of

Kent, and those subject to him, had profited from Christ's mercy and that he too could be granted that gift. The Pope denounced the worship of idols and offered Edwin deliverance from original sin and the evil of the devil, and a place in Heaven. The Pope also wrote at length to the Queen urging her to use her influence to convert Edwin. He asked her to reply as soon as possible with news of the conversion of the King and the people over whom he reigned. The Pope's gifts to the Queen were a silver mirror and a gold and ivory comb.

After some thought, Edwin told Paulinus that he would convert to Christianity but that he would first have to consult with the members of the Witan. Edwin summoned a meeting of the wise men and asked each of them in turn what they thought of Christianity and the new way of worshipping. The members of the Witan must have realized that Edwin intended to be baptized because, according to Bede, their praise of the new religion was fulsome, and their contempt for the Old Ways great. The Chief Wizard, Coifi, gave a speech which was critical of the Old Ways but less than enthusiastic about Christianity. It ended with him saying that he would accept the decision of the King. Another speaker made the famous speech in which he compared our passage through life to the flight of a sparrow through the King's hall on a winter's day. *"The bird flies in from the rain and snow of winter to briefly enjoy the warmth and safety of the hall before swiftly vanishing from sight into the wintry world from which it came. Likewise we know nothing of what precedes or follows life"*. It was argued that if the new religion brought knowledge of an after-life it should be followed. The other elders and advisers agreed and gave their support to the new religion.

Coifi, seeing how things were going, asked Paulinus to give a further and more detailed exposition of the Christian faith. When he had finished Coifi declared that he was convinced of the truth of the new doctrine which would bring salvation and eternal happiness to them all. He then proposed that the temples and altars of the Old Ways be desecrated and burned. When asked who should be the first to profane the altars and shrines of the idols, Coifi replied that he would do it himself and girded with a sword, and with a spear in his hand, he mounted a stallion and rode to the temple where he cast the spear into it, thus profaning it. Then Coifi instructed his companions to set fire to the temple and the enclosures surrounding it. The Chief Wizard had shown his commitment to the new order from the moment he took the sword as it was a sacrilege for him to carry a weapon or ride anything but a mare. This version of events is based on Bede's account and must therefore be seen as somewhat biased. It does however provide useful information.

Edwin was baptised at York on 12th April 627 but his new faith was unable to preserve him for long and in 633 he was defeated and killed in battle by the heathen Penda of Mercia and Cadwallon of Gwynedd.

The rulers of other kingdoms were gradually won over to the new faith but some conversions were half-hearted and there were setbacks for the Christian missionaries. Rædwald king of the East Engles (Angles) was apparently converted to Christianity during a visit to the court of King Ethelbert of Kent, but on his return home his wife and advisers undid the work. Rædwald was a pragmatist and it is likely that he feigned conversion knowing there were political benefits to be had from appeasing the Church and it may have been for this reason that he set up a Christian altar in his temple beside the heathen one. The heathen idols within Rædwald's temple were probably representations of the gods and just the sort of thing Pope Gregory had in mind when he wrote to King Edwin. The Pope attacked those who worshipped idols, quoted the psalms, and reminded Edwin that the idols have eyes but cannot see: ears but cannot hear: noses but cannot smell: hands but cannot feel: feet but cannot walk. *"We fail to understand how people can worship as gods objects which they have fashioned themselves to give the likeness of a body."* The Pope seems to have missed the point that heathens no more worshipped their idols than did Christians worship the crucifix. Rings, spears and sheaves of corn symbolized the gods in the same way that for Christians the cross came to symbolize Christ and the Church, and bread and wine symbolized the flesh and blood of Christ.

On the death of Ethelbert in 616 his son Eadbald came to the throne and quickly made it plain that he was a heathen. He married his stepmother (a heathen custom designed to maintain alliances and preserve continuity) much to the horror of the Church, but he did not force the bishops to leave his kingdom. Shortly afterwards the Christian King Sabert of the East Saxons (Essex) died and his three heathen sons inherited his kingdom and, according to Bede, they were quick to profess idolatry, which they had pretended to abandon during the lifetime of their father, and encouraged their people to follow the Old Ways. Bishop Mellitus refused to give them the backing of the Church unless they renounced their faith and were baptized, but he overestimated his strength and underestimated their determination, and he and his followers were ordered to leave the kingdom. Mellitus went first to Kent and then to Gaul, then returned after a year or two to try again, but the people of London refused to accept him back as Bishop apparently happy to continue to practise their heathen customs.

Christianity and Runes

The Church persisted with its attempts to bring the English into its sphere of influence and eventually it was successful. Once it had established Christianity as the official religion, the Church began extracting wealth from the kings and their subjects for the purpose of paying the clergy, building churches and setting up monasteries. In order to retain the support of the Church, and to win glory in heaven, the kings ceded to the Church large amounts of land and the rights to various forms of income. It has been suggested that the diversion of wealth to the Church undermined and weakened the relationship between the king and his warrior companions. The existence of an elite warrior class had been an important factor in enabling the English to defeat the Welsh and to retain the territory captured. That system, in simple terms, was based on a circulation of wealth. The king bestowed honours and gifts (including land) on his Companions and they fought for him and enabled the kingdom to grow. On the death of a Companion much of the wealth returned to the king and was available for redistribution to other Companions. When the Church acquired grants of land and rights to dues, and exemption from obligations, wealth was permanently lost to the system. A King gained recognition from the Church as being the legitimate ruler, under God, and the Church encouraged alliances of Christian kings against heathen kings. When all the kings had been converted it was in the interest of the Church to encourage stability and peace. This was fine provided all the kingdoms were part of the system and the only external threat was from the Welsh and the Gaels of Scotland but when the heathen Vikings invaded, the Church was unable to offer practical help and England was overrun, with one kingdom after another falling to a comparitively small force which in earlier times would have been easily dealt with. It was only due to King Alfred of Wessex, who rallied his warriors and won back his own kingdom, that England was saved. He laid the foundations of a strategy that came to fruition long after his death with the eventual defeat of the Danes and the supremacy, in Britain, of the English state under King Æthelstan.

An alternative explanation for the inability of the English kingdoms to successfully resist the Scandinavian invasions is that the English kingdoms had conquered all the land worth taking and the system that maintained a warrior elite had failed, as it was bound to do, because it depended on continual teritorial expansion. Against this it can be said that once the opportunities for expansion in Britain were exhausted, attention could have been directed abroad and the English may have attacked and brought parts of Scandinavia under their control. Instead the vigorous heathen warrior societies of Scandinavia attacked, and took control of, a large part of England.

That the old heathen virtues were not entirely ousted by Christianity is evident from Old English verse and in particular, *The Battle of Maldon,* which was written about one thousand years ago. The poem gives an account of a battle between an English army, probably drawn from Essex, and invading Vikings. The heathen values extolled in the poem may not have been much in evidence in England at the end of the 10th century, and the person recording the event may have been harking back to a time when they were.

The advocates of the new religion were not as tolerant as the followers of the Old Ways, and they quickly set about removing as many traces of the old customs as they could. That was not an easy task as the Old Ways showed greater concern for life in this world than the next, and the seasonal festivals were an important part of the life of the community. It is sometimes suggested that Christianity won converts by love and kindness, but there is little evidence of that. Churches were built on the sites of heathen temples or the temples were converted into churches. The Church took control of burial sites, and through their monopoly on performing naming ceremonies, weddings and funerals, the priests were able to gradually force the population to observe Christian customs. There were compromises of course but they were born out of necessity. For example, shortly after his arrival in Kent, Augustine wrote to Pope Gregory asking for guidance on several matters, one of which concerned the heathen practice, (a fairly common occurrence among kings), of a man marrying his stepmother or sister-in-law. The Pope's reply, in part, was that the people were not to be punished for sins they had unknowingly committed before baptism because, *"in these days the Church corrects some things strictly but allows others out of leniency; other transgressions are deliberately glossed over and tolerated, and by doing so the Church often succeeds in checking an evil of which she disapproves.*" However when the people were instructed in the faith they were to be warned that unlawful marriages were a grave offence and would incur the terrible judgement of God and the pains of eternal punishment.

The strategy of the Church was to get worshippers to accept change little by little and that was done by adapting the old customs from one generation to the next, so that new customs were introduced and heathen traditions gained a Christian veneer. The heathen festivals were given Christian connotations, but some festivals were so firmly linked with the seasons, the agricultural year and the Old Ways that their heathen names lingered on. Thanksgiving services were held but thanks were offered to the Christian god instead of Frig. The need to balance the Sky Father with the Earth Mother was later re-introduced in the form of the cult of the Virgin Mary.

The policy of adapting and modifying what already existed was clearly set out in a letter from Pope Gregory to Abbot Mellitus in 601. In it he asked Mellitus to inform Augustine that, after giving careful thought to the affairs of the English, it had been decided that on no account were the temples of the idols to be destroyed:

> *The idols are to be destroyed but the temples themselves are to be sprinkled with holy water and altars set up in them, and relics placed there. If the temples are well-built, they must be purified from devil-worship and dedicated to the service of the true God. In this way, it is to be hoped, the people, seeing that their temples have not been destroyed, will abandon their idolatry and continue to go to those places and come to know and revere the true God. And since it is their custom to sacrifice many oxen to the demons, let some other rite be substituted in its place such as a day of Dedications or the festivals of the holy martyrs whose relics are enshrined there. On such high days they might well build shelters of timber for themselves around the churches that were once temples and celebrate the occasion with devout feasting. They are no longer to sacrifice animals to the Devil, but they may kill them for food to the glory of God and give thanks to the Giver for the plenty they enjoy. . . . They are to offer the same animals as before but instead of offering them to idols they are to offer them to God, so that they should no longer be offering the same sacrifice.*

Many churches, certainly the older ones, were built on the sites of heathen temples and that would explain the association between ancient churchyards and yew trees, the holy tree of the heathen English. Evidence from Sweden supports the view that heathen temples probably had within their enclosure a tree or wooden pillar, and a spring, or well, or pool of water.

The letter from Pope Gregory indicates that the whole community came together in the temple enclosure on feast days to make sacrifices and to make merry. The custom of sacrificing many oxen to the gods and burning their bones on large fires (bonefires) probably took place during Bloodmonth (November).

The Springtide fertility festival named after the goddess *Eostre* has become Easter and its association with a symbol of birth and life, the egg, has not been lost. Yuletide is still one of the most important festivals of the year. The Yule-log custom, which symbolizes continuity, is still observed, and the heathen practice of tree worship, though once lost, was re-introduced to England from Germany as the Christmas tree, by Prince Albert, in Victorian times. Another aspect of tree worship lingers on with Maypoles which were decorated with flowers and leaves. Wooden pillars were probably also set up at shrines and may have been engraved with runes. In some places in the north of England, where stone was more readily available, such places were marked with a pillar of stone. Those monuments may have been the precursors of the market cross, such as that at Banbury. The Bewcastle column and the Ruthwell Cross (the cross may have been added to the pillar long after it was built) are examples of such monuments marked with runes. That the inscriptions on the Ruthwell Cross, which may date from the eighth century, survived to be recorded, is due to the Christians of the sixteenth and seventeenth centuries who set about destroying surviving heathen relics. The pillar was pulled down because it, and the runic inscription on it, were thought to be heathen. In fact the inscription records the crucifixion and is very similar to part of the Old English poem *The Dream of the Rood*. The pieces of the pillar were left lying on the ground and by good fortune that part of it that lay in the mud was well preserved. Many maypoles were also destroyed during the purges, the best known being the one that was erected each year in Leadenhall Street, London. The custom was banned in 1517 and about thirty years later the pole was cut up and burned after it had been denounced as an idol by a clergyman. The destruction of heathen wooden pillars was nothing new. On the orders of Charlemagne, in 772, a massive wooden pillar situated at Marsberg, a place of worship for the continental Saxons, was cut down and burned. The pillar was called Irminsul and was probably situated at the temple of Tanfana.

That the Church was less than tolerant when it became a powerful force in the land is evident from the following passage.

> *Clearly there was considerable effort expended by the Christians to obliterate entirely writings and monuments of the native past, and bury them in the everlasting grave of oblivion. For clearly they were convinced that as long as any trace of the culture and ancient signs obtruded on the minds of men, the business of conversion could not properly proceed, with men inclined and liable to return to their former errors. At the same time, so that the power of the darkness should not obstruct the rays of truth, nor on the other hand to make the common people too clever, above their capacity, a distinction of 'use' from 'abuse', and so that zeal for the word of the ministers, customary among the priests, should grow, and that enthusiasm for bringing the Roman Church to all minds grow too, it seemed wise to substitute Roman letters, as holier, for the letters of the Northmen, polluted as they were, by native superstition. On which point, my pronouncement is hardly required that I know it for certain but I freely maintain it.* (Stephanius, Not. Uber. p. 46. Translation Bill Griffiths)

It would appear that in England the Church was not altogether successful in suppressing heathenism despite there being punishments for the observance of various heathen customs (*c. VIII of the Penitential of Archbishop Egbert of York*). Alcuin wrote to Bishop Higbald of Lindisfarne in 797 with the message: " . . *let God's words be read in the refectory. There it is proper to listen to a lector, not a harpist, to the sermons of the Fathers, not the songs of the Heathen. For what has Ingeld to do with Christ?*'. (*Epistolae*, ed. Dummler 1895). Ingeld was Ing, God of Fertility. Various forms of the name are given in the genealogies of the English kings of Bernicia (in Northumbria) and indicate that there may be links between the English and the Vandals as the *Rune Poem* connects Ing with the Heardings who were the royal dynasty of the Vandals.

It is evident from the various codified laws that witches and various heathen customs and practices still existed long after England was nominally Christian. The very laws which sought to suppress heathenism helped preserve knowledge of its customs.

Punishments for heathens and others who turn from the Church of God. (c.690)

1. The Apostle says: 'Those who serve idols will not possess the kingdom of God.' Anyone who makes minor sacrifices to demons will do penance for one year; and for major sacrifices ten years.

2. If anyone, in ignorance, eats or drinks by a heathen shrine they are to promise never to do so again and to do forty days penance on bread and water. If it is deliberately done again, that is after a priest has declared that it is a sacrilege and the place a table of demons, the offender shall do penance on bread and water for thrice forty days. But if it is done to glorify the idol the penance shall be for three years.

3. If anyone sacrifices to demons for a second or third time they are to incur three years penance; then two years without any offering of communion. In the third five years, at the end of a five year period the offender is capable of perfection.

4. Anyone who eats what has been sacrificed to idols and was under no compulsion to do so is to fast for twelve weeks on bread and water; if it was done of necessity they are to fast for six weeks.

5. Anyone who feasts in the abominable places of the heathen by taking and eating their food there, should be subject to penance for two years, and be offered on probation for full two years, and after that be accepted to perfection; when offered, test the spirit and discuss the life of each individual.

6. If any do sacrilege, that is summon diviners who practice divination by birds, or any divination with evil intent, let them do penance for three years, one of which is to be on bread and water.

7. Christians are not allowed to leave the Church of God and go to divination, or name angels or make assemblies which are known to be forbidden. If any be found following this occult idolatry, in that they abandon our Lord Jesus Christ, the Son of God, and gave themselves to idolatry . . .

8. Clerks or laymen are not permitted to be sorcerers or enchanters, or to make amulets which are proved to be fetters for their souls; those who act thus are to be driven from the Church.

9. Those who injure a person by black magic are to do penance for seven years, three of these on bread and water.

10. If any use love potions but hurt nobody; if he is a layman he is to do penance for half a year; if he is a clerk one year on bread and water; if he is a subdeacon he is to do penance for two years, one year of which is to be on bread and water; if he

years with three on bread and water. If however by this means a woman is deceived about bringing forth, then he is to do a further three years penance on bread and water, lest he be accused of being a party to murder.

11. If any seek diviners whom they call prophets, or do any divinations, in that this is also diabolical, let them do penance for five years, three of these on bread and water.

12. If anyone takes lots, which are called contrary to the principals of the Saints, or takes any lots at all, or takes lots with evil intent, or makes divinations, let them do penance for three years, one of these on bread and water.

13. If any woman does divinations or diabolical incantations, let her do penance for one year, or thrice forty days, or forty days, according to the enormity of the crime of the penitent.

14. If any woman places her son or daughter on the roof for the sake of a cure or in an oven, let her do penance for seven years.

15. If any burn grain where a man has died for the sake of the living or of the house, let him do penance for five years on bread and water.

16. If any for the health of his young son should pass through a fissure in the ground and should close it after him with thorns, let him do penance for forty days on bread and water.

17. If any seek out divinations and pursue them in the manner of the heathen, or introduce men into their house for the purpose of finding something out by the evil arts or to make an expiation, let them be cast out if they be of the clergy; but if they are secular let them, after confession, be subject to five years penance, according to the rules ordained of old.

18. If any make or perform a vow at trees, or springs, or stones, or boundaries, or anywhere other than in the house of God, let him do penance for three years on bread and water. This is sacrilege or demonic. If any eat or drink there let him do penance for one year on bread and water.

19. If any go at the New Year as a young stag or cow, that is if he shares the habit of wild beasts and is dressed in the skins of cattle and puts on the heads of beasts, any who thus transform themselves into the likeness of beasts are to do three years penance.

20. Anyone who is an astrologer, that is someone who changes the mind of a man by invoking demons, is to do five years penance, one on bread and water.

21. Anyone who is a sender of storm, that is evil-doing, is to do seven years penance, three on bread and water.

22. Anyone who makes amulets, which is detestable, should do three years penance, one on bread and water.

23. Anyone who makes a habit of auguries and divinations is to do five years penance.

24. Anyone who observes soothsayers, or witchcrafts and devilish amulets and dreams and herbs, or who on the fifth day honours Jove [Thunor on Thursday] as do the heathen, is to do penance for five years if a clerk and three years if a layman.

25. Anyone who, when the moon is eclipsed, calls to her and practices witchcrafts to defend her in a sacrilegious manner, are to do penance for five years

26. Anyone who, in honour of the moon, goes hungry to bring about healing is to do penance for one year.

The Laws of Edward and Guthrum

OF WITCHES, DIVINERS, OATH-BREAKERS, &c.

11. If witches or diviners, oath-breakers or those who work secretly to destroy life, or foul, defiled, notorious adulteresses, be found anywhere within the land; let them be driven from the country and the people cleansed, or let them totally perish within the country, unless they desist, and very deeply atone.

The Laws of King Æthelstan (924-939)

OF WITCH-CRAFTS

6. And we have ordained respecting witchcrafts, and the giving of secret potions, and destruction-deeds: if any one should be thereby killed, and he who practised them could not deny it, that he be liable to his life. But if he will deny it, and at the threefold ordeal shall be guilty; that he be 120 days in prison: and after that let his kindred take him out, and give to the king 120 shillings, and pay compensation to the victims kindred, and stand surety for the murderer, that he evermore desist from the like.

The Laws of King Edmund (939-946)

OF OATH-BREAKERS AND SPELLWORKERS

6. Those who break oaths and work spells and make secret potions, let them be for ever cast out from all communion with God, unless they turn to right repentance.

Canons enacted under King Edgar (959-975)

16. And we enjoin, that every priest zealously promote Christianity, and totally extinguish every heathenism; and forbid well-worshipping, and spiritualism, and divinations, and enchantments, and idol-worshipping, and the vain practices which are carried on with various spells, and with peace-enclosures, and with elders, and also with various other trees, and with stones, and with many various delusions, with which men do much of what they should not.

18. And we enjoin, that on feast-days heathen songs and devil's games be abstained from.

The Laws of King Ethelred (978-1008)

6. And moreover we will beseech every friend, and all people who also diligently teach, that they, with inward heart, love one God, and carefully shun every heathenism.

7. And if witches or soothsayers, spellworkers or whores, or those who work secretly to destroy life or oathbreakers, be anywhere found in the country, let them diligently be driven out of this country, and this people be purified: or let them totally perish in the country, unless they desist, and the more deeply make atonement.

9. And it is the ordinance of the witan, that Christian men, and uncondemned persons, be not sold out of the country, at least not into a heathen nation; but let it be carefully guarded against, that those souls be not made to perish that Christ has brought with his own blood.

The Laws of King Cnut (1020-1023)

OF HEATHENISM

5. And we earnestly forbid every heathenism: heathenism is that men worship idols; that is, they worship heathen gods, and the sun or the moon, fire or rivers, water-wells or stones, or forest tree of any kind; or love witchcraft, or promote death-work in any wise; or by sacrifice, or by divination; or perform any thing pertaining to such illusions.

Laws for Northumbrian Priests (1020-1023)

47. We are all to worship and love one God, and zealously observe only Christianity, and every heathenship totally renounce.

48. If then anyone be found that shall henceforth practise any heathenship, either by sacrifice or by divination, or in any way love witchcraft, or worship idols, if he be a king's thane, let him pay 10 half-marks; half to Christ, half to the king.

54. If there be a peace-enclosure on any one's land, about a stone, or a tree, or a well, or any folly of such kind, then let him who made it pay a fine; half to Christ, half to the lord of the estate: and if the lord will not aid in levying the fine, then let Christ and the king have the compensation.

If the Church was so intent on obliterating, by various means, all traces of heathenism why is it that knowledge, and use, of runes persisted in monasteries, and that public monuments continued to be inscribed with runes? The Old English poem, *Solomon and Saturn,* and the Cynewulf poems contain runes, and the *Rune Poem* gives their meanings. The *thorn* and *wyn* runes were adopted as letters by the monks as there was no appropriate Roman letter to represent the relevant sounds in the Old English language.

A possible explanation is that knowledge of runes was so widespread that the Church could not ignore them, and so it adapted them for its own use and, by Christianizing them, managed to change their meaning and significance. Another possibility is that wizards and all traces of the heathenism they adhered to was so completely destroyed that monks were able to use runes as an anachronistic curiosity, a kind of private joke. Kemble suggested another explanation.

. . how are we to account for the undeniable fact, that at the very earliest period these characters were used in England for Christian inscriptions? It seems to me that the only way of solving this intricate problem, is to assume, that the earliest converts were the priests themselves; which fact, astounding as it is, is rendered probable by positive evidence. If this were the case, they who knew what the Runes really were, might have the less scruple in using them, with or without the Roman characters. And, as nearly every inscription we have must be referred to Northumberland, we find this the more intelligible, when we bear in mind, that before the close of the eighth century Northumberland was more advanced in civilization than any other portion of Teutonic Europe.

(Kemble, *Anglo-Saxon Runes*)

What reason might the Church have for recruiting wizards? The answer might lie in the practical organizational problems involved in a switch from one religion to another. Pope Gregory's letter indicates a desire for continuity and gradual transition so as not to alarm the people unduly. It was not a matter of tolerance but one of practicality. If, as seems certain, a gradual change in the use of spells, festivals and buildings was part of the process of gaining control, why not also make use of the wizards as they were the most important part of the structure. They knew the charms and spells; they were literate; and they were the most highly educated people in that society. Wizards and witches used runes, and were responsible for adapting existing runes and creating new ones to meet the needs of a changing language. They had a knowledge of starcraft, festivals, laws and customs, and the wizards who officiated at moots knew the local land boundaries. If this assessment is correct, wizards were an administrative class that would today be called 'civil servants'. In addition, they had direct contact with the people through their supervision of ceremonies. The people would be more likely to accept change if it came from a priest they knew than from a stranger. The hierarchy of the Church in England was sent from Rome but wizards may have been incorporated into the system as priests and have performed a similar function to the one they had before. The advantages to them from this change were not just those to do with keeping their jobs, and their income, but the positive ones associated with gaining access to the resources of a centralized international organization. The motto of such priests may have been, 'if you can't beat them join them'. Perhaps some did take to Christianity with enthusiasm born of conviction, but it is probable that many retained their heathen beliefs and customs which they secretly practised.

When the Church gained power it did not attempt to suppress magical practices; its aim was instead to suppress heathen magical practices. As we have seen Christians set about modifying heathen customs to make them appear Christian. Spells retained their heathen roots and structure but were said in church and called prayers. Bishops and archbishops took the place of wizards as advisers to kings, and every opportunity was taken to show that Christian magic was stronger than that of the Old Ways, with the Church claiming the credit for good fortune and blaming the gods of the Old Ways, who were now called devils, and their followers, for any misfortune. An example of Christians claiming their magic to be stronger than heathen magic, can be found with Bede (*A History of the English Church and People*) who told the story of a nobleman who had been wounded in battle, and lain unconscious amongst the bodies of the dead. When he revived he was taken prisoner, and chained at night to prevent his escape but every morning he was found to be free of his bonds. His captor believed that this was due to the nobleman, *having about him the letters of unbinding, the sort about which stories are told.* (i.e. runes). Bede however claimed that the reason the fetters fell from the nobleman was that his brother, an abbot, said Mass for him each evening.

Another of the many examples of Christian magic is the story, again told by Bede, of how Mellitus, the third Archbishop of Canterbury, saved Canterbury from complete destruction by fire. The raging flames were sweeping towards his residence, having already destroyed a large area of the city. The frail bishop ordered that he be carried out and placed in the path of the flames and there by his prayers (spells) he averted the danger that stronger men had been powerless to check. The wind changed direction, blowing the flames back, and then stilled so that the fires burned out. The Church was clearly in a position to propagate many such stories in the knowledge that those who dared to deny the truth of the tales could be labelled the agents of the devil.

But what of those who did not wish to give up their faith; what became of them? During the early stages of Christian expansion in England the conversion of a king to Christianity did not necessarily win over his heirs, and presumably they retained wizards as their advisers. Other wizards may have lived as hermits or travellers making use of any skills that they might have that were of use to ordinary people. Some went to other kingdoms but it is probable that many wizards had no wish to give up their homeland or their faith, and actively resisted the growing power of the Church with the only weapon they had, and that was magic.

Summary

Witches and wizards were respected members of heathen society. They were probably healers (herbalists), soothsayers, midwives, psychologists, magicians, keepers of the laws, and keepers of the calendar. They officiated at festivals, and at ceremonies connected with the passage through life, such as birth, coming-of-age, wedding (handfasting) and death. Witchcraft encompassed a very large body of knowledge and out of necessity there was specialization. Because of the nature of the society, and the differing real and perceived aptitudes and qualities of men and women, they tended to specialize in different areas of their craft. As with other crafts of that time, the knowledge and skills possessed by witches was passed on through families for the reason that specialist information provided the opportunity to earn a living and in many cases gave status and power to those who possessed it. Witches and wizards would probably have learnt the craft from their mother or father but it is also likely that new entrants were admitted to the craft, perhaps through a process determined by a coven or some other such grouping.

If there was specialization in the form suggested, it might indicate a tendency for witches to work in groups and for wizards to be more solitary figures. Taking this somewhat tenuous line of reasoning one step further, it might be suggested that witches sought enlightenment and contact with the Earth Mother and Sky Father through group activities, while wizards tended towards shamanistic methods and techniques.

The involvement of wizards in the process of government gave them power and influence but also made them vulnerable when kings, for political purposes, converted to Christianity. The wizards had to choose between retaining their jobs by becoming priests in the new religious order, or of losing their influence, status and livelihood. Some wizards were probably unwilling to compromise their beliefs and operated in much the same way as witches, while others lived as hermits or travellers. Witches on the other hand were more secure because the vast majority of the population adhered to the Old Ways long after the ruling elites converted to the new, alien religion, and witches provided an essential service to the communities in which they lived. Another factor that may have helped witches survive the arrival of Christianity was that the Church could not offer a direct replacement for them as it was unable to recruit witches as priestesses.

Although witches and wizards fulfilled important roles in society and, in the case of witches, had considerable contact with members of their local community, it does not mean that they were treated as any other person who provided a service. Because of the nature of the service they knew a great deal about their neighbours and that knowledge, combined with their various skills, probably meant that they were held in some awe and fear by much of the population. Bede, when describing the meeting in the Isle of Thanet between King Ethelbert and Augustine in 597, mentions that the King summoned Augustine and his companions to an audience in the open air because he held a heathen superstition that if they were practitioners of magic and met him in a house they might have the opportunity to deceive and master him. If the King was wary of the practitioners of magic it is reasonable to suppose that others had similar fears.

The Hallowing of England
A Guide to the Saints of Old England and their Places of Pilgrimage

Fr. Andrew Philips

In the Old English period we can count over 300 saints, yet today their names and exploits are largely unknown. They are part of a forgotten England which, though it lies deep in the past, is an important part of our national and spiritual history.

Although the holy relics of the saints and the churches they built are long gone, the sites where they laboured are still here and their presence can still be sensed in those places hallowed by these saints. Each journey through our land can, if we so choose, become a pilgrimage.

This guide includes a list of saints, an alphabetical list of places with which they are associated, and a calendar of saint's feast days.

UK £4·95 net   ISBN 1-898281-08-4   96pp

Sixty Saxon Saints

Alan Smith

Alan Smith has produced a useful concise guide which contains biographical details of most of the better known English saints and a calendar of their feast days.

The purpose of this booklet is to see some justice done to the English saints of the Anglo-Saxon period who took with them from the secular into the religious life the native English ideals of loyalty to one's Lord and, if necessary, sacrificial service to his cause.

This selection of saints includes some who were not of native birth but who are important to the story of English Christianity.

UK £2-95 net   ISBN 1-898281-07-6   48pp

Spellcraft
Old English Heroic Legends

Kathleen Herbert

The author has taken the skeletons of ancient Germanic legends about great kings, queens and heroes, and put flesh on them. Kathleen Herbert's extensive knowledge of the period is reflected in the wealth of detail she brings to these tales of adventure, passion, bloodshed and magic.

The book is in two parts. First are the stories that originate deep in the past, yet because they have not been hackneyed, they are still strange and enchanting. After that there is a selection of the source material, with information about where it can be found and some discussion about how it can be used. The purpose of the work is to bring pleasure to those studying Old English literature and, more importantly, to bring to the attention of a wider public the wealth of material that has yet to be tapped by modern writers, composers and artists.

Kathleen Herbert is the author of a trilogy, set in sixth century Britain, that includes a winner of the Georgette Heyer prize for an outstanding historical novel.

UK £6·95 net US $14·95 ISBN 0-9516209-9-1 292pp

Rune Cards

Tony Linsell and Brian Partridge

This package, which has received widespread acclaim, provides all that is needed for anyone to learn how to read runes. The thirty cards are accompanied by a ninety-two page booklet which gives background information about runes and, clearly and concisely, explains how to use them.

> *This boxed set of 30 cards contains some of the most beautiful and descriptive black and white line drawings that I have ever seen on this subject.*   Pagan News

> *These are fantastic....Real magic, fabulous and brooding imagery, and an easy doorway to runic realms....*   Occult Observer

> *There is a thick little book which includes clear and concise instructions on how to cast the runes. It is detailed without being overbearing and Mr Linsell obviously knows his stuff.....*   Clamavi

The illustrations on the cards include prompts that will quickly enable the user to read the runes without referring to the book.

UK £12·95 net   US $19·95   ISBN 0-9516209-7-5   30 cards + 92pp booklet

---

Looking for the Lost Gods of England

Kathleen Herbert

Kathleen Herbert sifts through the royal genealogies, charms, verse and other sources to find clues to the names and attributes of the Gods and Goddesses of the early English. The earliest account of English heathen practices reveals that they worshipped the Earth Mother and called her Nerthus. The names Tiw, Woden, Thunor, and Frig have been preserved in place names and in the names given to days of the week. The tales, beliefs and traditions of that time are still with us and able to stir our minds and imaginations; they have played a part in giving us *A Midsummer Night's Dream* and the *Lord of the Rings*.

Kathleen Herbert is the author of a trilogy, set in sixth century Britain, that includes a winner of the Georgette Heyer prize for an outstanding historical novel.

UK £4·95 net   ISBN 1-898281-04-1   64pp

The Battle of Maldon
Text and Translation

Translated and edited by Bill Griffiths

The Battle of Maldon was fought between the Englishmen of Essex and the Vikings in AD 991. The action was captured in an Anglo-Saxon poem whose vividness and heroic spirit has fascinated readers and scholars for generations. *The Battle of Maldon* includes the source text; edited text; parallel literal translation; verse translation; review of 103 books and articles.

UK £4·95 net   US $14·95   ISBN 0-9516209-0-8   96pp

Wordcraft
Concise English/Old English Dictionary and Thesaurus

Stephen Pollington

This book provides Old English equivalents to the commoner modern words in both dictionary and thesaurus formats.

Previously the lack of an accessible guide to vocabulary deterred many would-be students of Old English. Now this book combines the core of indispensable words relating to everyday life with a selection of terms connected with society, culture, technology, religion, perception, emotion and expression to encompass all aspects of Anglo-Saxon experience.

The Thesaurus presents vocabulary relevant to a wide range of individual topics in alphabetical lists, thus making it easily accessible to those with specific areas of interest. Each thematic listing is encoded for cross-reference from the Dictionary. The two sections will be of invaluable assistance to students of the language, as well as to those with either a general or a specific interest in the Anglo-Saxon period.

UK £9·95 net US $19·95 ISBN 1–898281–02–5 256pp

Alfred's Metres of Boethius

Edited by Bill Griffiths

In this new edition of the Old English *Metres of Boethius*, clarity of text, informative notes and a helpful glossary have been a priority, for this is one of the most approachable of Old English verse texts, lucid and delightful; its relative neglect by specialists will mean this text will come as a new experience to many practised students of the language; while its clear, expositional verse style makes it an ideal starting point for all amateurs of the period.

In these poems, King Alfred re-built the Latin verses from Boethius' *De Consolatione Philosophiae* ("On the Consolation of Philosophy") into new alliterative poems, via an Old English prose intermediary. The stirring images and stories of Boethius' original are retained – streams, legends, animals, volcanoes – and developed for an Anglo-Saxon audience to include the Gothic invasion of Italy (Metre 1), the figure of Welland the Smith (Metre 10), and the hugely disconcerting image of Death's hunt for mankind (Metre 27). The text is in effect a compendium of late classical science and philosophy, tackling serious issues like the working of the universe, the nature of the soul, the morality of power – but presented in so clear and lively a manner as to make it as challenging today as it was in those surprisingly Un-Dark Ages.

Texts are in Old English with a Modern English Introduction and notes

UK £14·95 net US $25 ISBN 1–898281–03–3 B5 208pp

Anglo-Saxon Verse Charms, Maxims and Heroic Legends

Louis J Rodrigues

The Germanic tribes who settled in Britain during the fifth and early sixth centuries brought with them a store of heroic and folk traditions: folk-tales, legends, rune-lore, magic charms, herbal cures, and the homely wisdom of experience enshrined in maxims and gnomic verse. In the lays composed and sung by their minstrels at banquets, they recalled the glories of long-dead heroes belonging to their Continental past. They carved crude runic inscriptions on a variety of objects including memorial stones, utensils, and weapons. In rude, non-aristocratic, verse, they chanted their pagan charms to protect their fields against infertility, and their bodies against the rigours of rheumatic winters. And, in times of danger, they relied on the gnomic wisdom of their ancestors for help and guidance.

Louis Rodrigues looks at those heroic and folk traditions that were recorded in verse, and which have managed to survive the depredations of time.

UK £7·95 net US $14·95 ISBN 1-898281-01-7 176pp

A Handbook of Anglo-Saxon Food
Processing and Consumption

Ann Hagen

For the first time information from various sources has been brought together in order to build up a picture of how food was grown, conserved, prepared and eaten during the period from the beginning of the 5th century to the 11th century. No specialist knowledge of the Anglo-Saxon period or language is needed, and many people will find it fascinating for the views it gives of an important aspect of Anglo-Saxon life and culture. In addition to Anglo-Saxon England the Celtic west of Britain is also covered. There is a comprehensive index.

UK £7·95 net US $16·95 ISBN 0-9516209-8-3 200pp

Beowulf: Text and Translation
Translated by John Porter

The verse in which the story unfolds is, by common consent, the finest writing surviving in Old English, a text that all students of the language and many general readers will want to tackle in the original form. To aid understanding of the Old English, **a literal word-by-word translation** by John Porter is printed opposite an edited text and provides a practical key to this Anglo-Saxon masterpiece.

UK £7·95 net US $16·95 ISBN 0-9516209-2-4 192pp

Anglo-Saxon Runes

John. M. Kemble

Kemble's essay *On Anglo-Saxon Runes* first appeared in the journal *Archaeologia* for 1840; it draws on the work of Wilhelm Grimm, but breaks new ground for Anglo-Saxon studies in his survey of the Ruthwell Cross and the Cynewulf poems. It is an expression both of his own indomitable spirit and of the fascination and mystery of the Runes themselves, making one of the most attractive introductions to the topic.

For this edition, new notes have been supplied, which include translations of Latin and Old English material quoted in the text, to make this key work in the study of runes more accessible to the general reader.

UK £6·95 net US $14·95 ISBN 0–9516209–1–6 80pp

The Service of Prime from the Old English Benedictine Office

Text and Translation – Prepared by Bill Griffiths

The Old English Benedictine Office was a series of monastic daily services compiled in the late tenth or early eleventh centuries from the material that had largely already been translated from Latin into Old English.

UK £2·50 net ISBN0–9516209–3–2 40pp

Monasteriales Indicia
The Anglo-Saxon Monastic Sign Language

Edited with notes and translation by
Debby Banham

The *Monasteriales Indicia* is one of very few texts which let us see how life was really lived in monasteries in the early Middle Ages. Written in Old English and preserved in a manuscript of the mid-eleventh century, it consists of 127 signs used by Anglo-Saxon monks during the times when the Benedictine Rule forbade them to speak. These indicate the foods the monks ate, the clothes they wore, and the books they used in church and chapter, as well as the tools they used in their daily life, and persons they might meet both in the monastery and outside. The text is printed here with a parallel translation. The introduction gives a summary of the background, both historical and textual, as well as a brief look at the later evidence for monastic sign language in England. Extensive notes provide the reader with details of textual relationships, explore problems of interpretation, and set out the historical implications of the text.

UK £6·95 net US $14·95 ISBN 0–9516209–4–0 96pp

An Introduction to
The Old English Language and its Literature

Stephen Pollington

The purpose of this general introduction to Old English is not to deal with the teaching of Old English but to dispel some misconceptions about the language and to give an outline of its structure and its literature. Some basic knowledge of these is essential to an understanding of the early period of English history and the present form of the language.

UK £2·95 net   ISBN 1–898281–06–8

Titles being worked on (August 1994) for publication:

English Martial Arts by Terry Brown

Early English Laws by Bill Griffiths

An Index to the Homilies by Robert DiNapoli

Alicc's Adventures in Wonderland illustrated by Brian Partridge

Anglo Saxon Food & Drink: Production & Distribution by Ann Hagen

For a full list of publications please send a s.a.e. to:

Anglo-Saxon Books
25 Malpas Drive, Pinner, MiddlesexHA5 1DQ England
Tel: 081-868 1564

In **North America** most titles can be ordered from bookshops or from our distributor:

Paul & Company Publishers Consortium Inc.
c/o PCS Data Processing Inc.,
360 West 31 St., New York, NY 10001
Tel: (212) 564-3730 ext. 264

Þa Engliscan Gesiðas

Þa Engliscan Gesiðas (The English Companions) is a historical and cultural society exclusively devoted to Anglo-Saxon history. Its aims are to bridge the gap between scholars and non-experts, and to bring together all those with an interest in the Anglo-Saxon period, its language, culture, and traditions, so as to promote a wider interest in, and knowledge of all things Anglo-Saxon. The Fellowship publishes a journal, *Wiðowinde*, which helps members to keep in touch with current thinking on topics from art and archaeology to heathenism and Early English Christianity. The Fellowship enables like-minded people to keep in contact by publicising conferences, courses and meetings that might be of interest to its members. A correspondence course in Old English is also available.

For further details write to:

The English Companions
BM Box 4336, London WC1N 3XX, England.

Regia Anglorum

Regia Anglorum is a society that was founded to accurately re-create the life of the British people as it was around the time of the Norman invasion of England. Its work has a strong educational slant and it considers authenticity to be of prime importance. Regia Anglorum prefers, where possible, to work from archaeological materials and is extremely cautious regarding such things as the interpretation of styles depicted in manuscripts. Approximately twenty-five per cent of its membership, of over 500 people, are archaeologists or historians.

The Society has a large working Living History Exhibit, teaching and exhibiting more than twenty crafts in an authentic environment. It owns a forty foot wooden ship replica of a type that would have been a common sight in Northern European waters around the turn of the first millennium AD. Battle re-enactment is another aspect of the Societies activities, often involving 200 or more warriors.

For further information contact:

K. J. Siddorn, 9 Durleigh Close, Headley Park, Bristol BS13 7NQ, England.

West Stow Anglo-Saxon Village

An early Anglo-Saxon Settlement reconstructed on the site where it was excavated consisting of timber and thatch hall, houses and workshop. Open all year 10a.m. – 4.15p.m. (except Yule). Free taped guides. Special provision for school parties. A teachers' resource pack is available. Costumed events are held at weekends, especially Easter Sunday and August Bank Holiday Monday. Craft courses are organised.

Details available from:

The Visitor Centre, West Stow Country Park
Icklingham Road, West Stow,
Bury St Edmunds, Suffolk IP28 6HG
Tel: 0284 728718

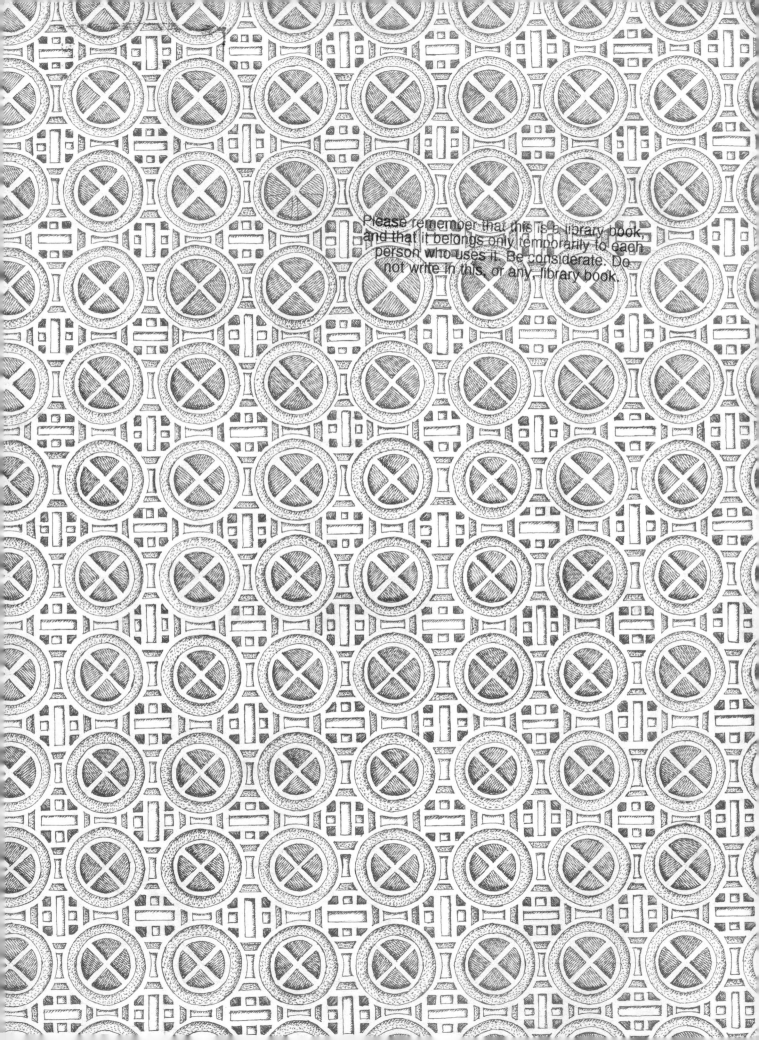